PARADISE LOST

PARADISE LOST

A NOVEL BY

KATE BRIAN

SIMON PULSE

New York   London   Toronto   Sydney

SIMON PULSE
An imprint of Simon & Schuster Children's Publishing Division
1230 Avenue of the Americas, New York, NY 10020

alloyentertainment
Produced by Alloy Entertainment
151 West 26th Street, New York, NY 10001

Typography by Andrea C. Uva
The text of this book was set in Filosofia.

Manufactured in the United States of America
First Simon Pulse paperback edition February 2009

2 4 6 8 10 9 7 5 3 1

Library of Congress Control Number 2008940132

ISBN-13: 978-1-4169-5884-0
ISBN-10: 1-4169-5884-3

For my sister, Erin, who is really going to love me after this

REALITY

Not happening. This was not happening.

I walked down the hall of the ICU at Edward Billings Memorial Hospital, trying to look as if I belonged there. Holding my coat closed tightly over my now ridiculous-seeming gold minidress and trying to make the nurses and doctors believe I knew where I was going. But I didn't. I didn't know where I was going, or where I was, or how I'd gotten there. I had never navigated these sterile halls, never had to visit this cold, ominous place with its grim-faced orderlies and somber lighting. The one thing I knew was that this could not be happening.

In my mind's eye, all I could see was the blood. I had woken up on the floor of the solarium in Mitchell Hall, the back of my head throbbing with pain. Noelle had been hosting a preparty there for Kiran Hayes's birthday fête in Boston, and I had gone to confront Sabine DuLac about her relationship with Ariana Osgood. She had pulled a gun on me, I had blacked out, and when I'd come to, I had seen Josh's prone body, his face pressed into the hardwood floor. And blood. Blood everywhere. The scream that had escaped my throat had sounded otherworldly, like something out of a science fiction film. Like nothing that could have come from my own throat. That was when Sabine had realized the bullet had missed me. Even though the gun was gone, even though Trey Prescott and Gage Coolidge were holding her back, she had made one final lunge, intent on strangling me or clawing my hair out—hurting me in whatever way possible. I had thrown myself backward in fear and had bumped into something hard. A second body. Dark hair had been splayed everywhere, arms bent at unnatural angles. Another scream, and after that, everything had become a blur.

The shouting as the police had hauled off Sabine. The Pemberly girl who, splattered with blood, had fainted dead away. The flashing lights of the ambulance. The EMTs shouting for us to stay back as they'd sorted out who was hit and who was unconscious and who might be . . . dead.

Now an orderly shoved a meal cart out of a room and right into my path. I was so startled that my hand flew to my heart. My knees felt like they could collapse at any second. I pressed my other palm against the wall to steady myself, my fingers landing just above a gold plate with a room number printed on it: 4005. Which meant that the next room was 4007. The room I was looking for. The room I dreaded.

Deep breath, Reed. You can do this. You have to do this.

I closed my eyes for a moment. This wasn't about me. Yes, Sabine had tried to kill me. Yes, the person who, all semester long, I had thought was my best friend had turned out to be a raving homicidal lunatic stalker. Yes, I had spent months living in the same room with a girl who had then tortured me and drugged me and sent out a lewd video of me to the entire Easton Academy community. *That* was all about me. And I could deal with all of that later.

But right now. This. This was not about me.

I took that deep breath and stepped tentatively into room 4007.

Josh's eyes instantly met mine, whisking the breath right out of me. I was aware of the machines—the beeping of the heart monitor, the strange twitching lines on the screen, the dripping IV. But for a moment, just one moment, all I could see were those eyes. The relief, the anguish, the longing, the fear. Everything I felt was right there in his eyes. He knew. He understood. But then he broke eye contact, and I dropped back to reality.

Reality, where Ivy Slade lay on a hospital bed, unconscious and pale, her eyelids appearing purple under the fluorescent lights. Tubes and wires and sensors were stuck to her temples and wrists, and her black hair was shoved back from her face in a haphazard, unparted way that she would have loathed if she could have seen it. The white hospital sheets were tightly tucked in all around her, giving her the look of a half-wrapped mummy. Only her arms were free, and Josh was holding her hand. Her delicate, seemingly lifeless hand. My throat went completely dry.

Why hadn't she stayed outside like the police had told her to do? Why had she run back into the solarium? In all the panic, I hadn't even realized that she had come up behind me. She didn't have to be there. Didn't have to come with me to confront Sabine. I had even told her not to come along, but she obviously was worried about me in my one-track state of mind. That track being the express train to confrontation with a homicidal maniac.

It was my fault that she was here. All my fault.

"Is she going to be okay?" I whispered.

Please say yes. Please, please say yes. I wasn't sure I could handle another death. Another funeral. Another good-bye. I wasn't sure if any of us could handle it.

"They think so," Josh replied. He looked hopefully over at her. "The bullet went through her upper shoulder and just missed her lung. If it had been half an inch lower . . . She lost a lot of blood, though, which is why she's unconscious right now. But yeah, they expect her to make a full recovery."

My eyes misted over as a crushing weight was lifted from my shoulders. She was going to be okay. *Thank you, thank you, thank you!* Ivy and I had just started to become friends. If it weren't for her, I may have never figured out that it was Sabine who was after me. That Sabine was the person who had killed Cheyenne Martin and had tried to make me believe it was my fault.

If it weren't for Ivy, I might have gone to Kiran's party with Sabine and ended up shot dead in an alley in Boston somewhere. Who knew what the details of the girl's plan had been? It seemed that, as long as it had ended with me dead, Sabine would have deemed it a success.

Josh placed Ivy's hand on the bed next to her hip and slowly got up to usher me out the door. As we left the room, I turned to him, prepared to be a good friend—a supportive friend and nothing more. To ask the right questions. The questions that Noelle Lange and Rose Sakowitz and all the other people down in the waiting room wanted me to ask. But before I could even open my mouth, I was in his arms.

"I thought she was going to kill you," he said breathlessly.

Surprised tears jumped to my eyes. I savored the familiar strength of his arms, the crisp scent of his shampoo. I clung to him, gripping the smooth fabric of his oxford shirt like it was a life vest and I was about to go under.

"I can't believe what you did," I said as a tear spilled down my cheek. "Lunging for the gun like that . . ." I forced myself to pull back so I could look into his eyes. "When you hit the floor, I thought you were dead."

Josh placed his hands on either side of my face and looked at me as if he was trying to reassure himself that I was actually there. "I didn't even think. You were frozen, and there was a gun pointing at you, and I . . . I didn't even think. It was either throw you down or go for the gun, and I guess I was closer to the gun, so . . . I just did it."

"You saved my life," I said, a sob choking my throat.

He moved his hands to cup my shoulders and touched his forehead to mine, blowing out a sigh. "You're okay. You're okay," he said. "Thank God you're okay."

Just like that, my heart filled with bubbles of joy. Josh still loved me. He loved me so much that he couldn't stop touching me. He loved me so much he had put himself in harm's way to save me. Josh loved me. I felt so high, I could have floated right out the hospital window.

But then, reality. Like a lasso around my ankle, reality once again slammed me back down to the ground. Because Josh's attempt to save my life had resulted in Ivy's current state. He had knocked the gun just as it had gone off. Knocked it so that the bullet had passed me by . . . and had hit Ivy right in the chest.

In trying to save me, his ex-girlfriend, Josh had put his current girlfriend in the hospital.

We both looked over at Ivy's room. I knew that Josh was thinking exactly what I was thinking, that Ivy didn't deserve this. He let his hands slip from my shoulders, and he stepped away. Suddenly, I was freezing. For the first time, I noticed the bloodstains on the front of his shirt. On his hands. Under his fingernails. Ivy's blood. It was everywhere.

"What happened to Sabine?" he asked flatly, as we started walking back to the waiting room.

"They arrested her," I told him. "Pretty much everyone heard her confess, so . . ."

"I can't believe this. I can't believe this is happening."

Josh pressed the heels of his hands into his eyes. I knew the feeling. It was all so overwhelming that it was hard to decide which part to try to sort out first. Cheyenne's pointless murder, Ivy's pointless injury, or the fact that Sabine was Ariana's sister and, apparently, had come to Easton for the sole purpose of torturing me. How were we supposed to deal with that?

And then, of course, there was the issue of us. The "us" that now included three: me, Josh, and Ivy.

"So . . . now we just . . . ," I trailed off. I knew Josh well enough to know that he always did the right thing. And the right thing at this moment did not include me.

We turned the corner and stopped down the hall from the waiting room. Josh leaned against the cinderblock wall. He looked miserable. Tired and gaunt and haunted. He raised his hands to his face again, making a little tent around his nose and mouth. For a moment, neither of us breathed. Then he dropped his hands, as if resolved, and looked at me. The emotion was gone. In its place was an expressionless wall.

"I have to stay with Ivy," he said firmly. "I have to know she's okay. She's going to need . . . someone."

My heart contracted painfully, and I allowed myself one moment of selfishness. One. *But what about me?* I thought. And then I let it go. Because he was right. Ivy needed him more than I did. Yes, I had been through a lot this semester. We both had. Cheyenne's murder, our breakup, my falling-out with Noelle, and the constant feeling that someone was stalking me. All the heartache and paranoia had been because of Sabine. It had all been part of her little "torture Reed for hurting Ariana" plan.

I wished that Josh and I could have talked through all of this right then. That we could have sat together and figured out what it all meant. But at that moment, it all meant nothing. Because he cared for Ivy and, as much pain as I was in, Ivy needed him more.

I glanced over my shoulder toward the waiting room. I saw Noelle hovering, watching me expectantly. We hadn't even had a conversation yet. Hadn't cleared the air after our massive breakup and her kicking me out of Billings. But she had made a peace offering—she'd invited me to the party tonight—and after everything we'd been through in the past few hours, I knew that things were going to go back to normal between us. At least I hoped they were. She was all I had now.

"I guess I should go tell them what's going on," I said slowly.

The last thing I wanted to do was leave him, but I had to. Standing in front of Josh and not being able to touch him was going to kill me.

"Okay," he replied, his eyes wet.

"Okay," I repeated, somehow getting the word past the lump in my throat.

I turned and started down the hall, my footsteps heavy. A few doors down, I paused and looked over my shoulder. He was still standing there, watching me. Watching me walk away from him. "Keep me posted, okay? On how she's doing."

"I promise."

So there it was. Good-bye. I was going to be strong. I was not going to pine and whine and wish. I was going to be good. For me, for Josh, and for Ivy. That was my promise to myself.

THE CRAZIES

Sunday morning, the sky was the perfect shade of gray. The kind that wouldn't bring the joy of snow, but would hang around all day, reminding everyone to be cold, down, depressed.

It was freezing inside the chapel. We all pulled our coats tighter as we stepped through the arched doorway and under the vaulted ceiling. The atmosphere was hushed. Whispers skittered along the cold stone floor and up the walls. We may as well have been attending a funeral in the austere old church. The girls of Pemberly gathered in their pews, hugging one another and resting their heads on each other's shoulders. Gage trudged in, head down, hands in the pockets of his heather gray coat. That was when I knew for sure that he was seriously depressed—the boy never wore outerwear. Thought he was too cool for bundling. But today his head was clearly somewhere else—room 4007.

"Students, let's all take our seats," Headmaster Cromwell said, stepping up to the podium.

I glanced at Diana Waters, my friend from Pemberly. Cromwell had never greeted us so informally before. As we sat down next to each other, I noticed that even his appearance had changed. He wore a burgundy wool sweater under his suit jacket and no tie. No American flag tie tack. It was Casual Crom.

"Freaky," Diana whispered as everyone settled in around us.

"No doubt," I replied.

"I'll make this short," Headmaster Cromwell began, his pale hands gripping either side of the podium. "First, as of today, I will be relinquishing my post as headmaster of Easton Academy."

Surprised murmurs filled the room.

"No more Crom?" Lorna Gross said from the pew behind mine. She actually sounded upset. I, however, felt a huge sense of relief, though it was tinged by irritation. I detested the Crom. He had put us all through the wringer this semester. But that also was part of the reason I was irritated. All those hoops I had jumped through for him . . . and now, next semester, there was going to be some new headmaster to suck up to.

Cromwell held up a hand to silence the crowd. "But I do have a few announcements to make before I go," he said. "First, due to the events of last night, the school will be breaking early for the holiday. Which means you are all excused from your finals."

This announcement was met with stunned silence. I was sure that a few of my classmates wanted to celebrate—I could practically feel the strain as they held back whoops of joy like a hundred overfilled helium balloons—but no one uttered a sound. Considering that Ivy was in the hospital, that yet another of our classmates had turned out to be a murderer, celebrating just didn't seem appropriate.

"The Board of Directors has discussed the situation, and we all believe that it would be best for you students to take this time to be with your families while the Board discusses how we might better ensure the security of the student body."

"He sounds like he's issuing a statement to the press," Diana whispered, tucking her hands under her arms.

"He's practicing," Missy Thurber said, leaning in from behind us. "Did you see the vultures parked outside the gates this morning? The press smells blood in the water, and they're about to chow down."

"You're mixing your metaphors again, Missy," I scolded through my teeth. When I glanced over my shoulder, I found myself staring into those yawning nostrils of hers. *Ick.*

"Whatever. I wouldn't be surprised if they shut down this place," Missy replied, sitting back again. "Parents have been calling all night. People are freaked out. *I'm* freaked out. I mean, I lived down the hall from the girl."

Yeah, and I'm the one who had a gun pointed at her head last night. Boo-freaking-hoo, Nostril Girl.

"Thank you for your time and attention," Mr. Cromwell said awkwardly. "You're all dismissed."

The room filled with chatter and exhausted-yet-exhilarated students jammed the aisles. I found Noelle as quickly as I could. She was on her way out the door with Amberly Carmichael and Tiffany Goulbourne, her long black coat contrasting sharply with Tiff's pristine white jacket. Amberly wore a light-blue coat with white gloves and a white hat and looked like a little American Girl doll. I felt a rush of anger at the sight of her—at the girl who'd taken my place in Billings and had ransacked my Pemberly single—but I did my best to push it back down.

"Noelle, wait!" I called, jogging to catch up.

They paused just outside the door and waited. Each had her cell phone out and ready, probably to spread the news that we'd been freed.

"Hey," Noelle said, pushing her dark hair over her shoulder. "Crazy stuff."

"I know," I replied, catching my breath. "Missy said they might close the school for good."

"Close Easton?" Amberly gasped, her blue eyes wide. "Can they do that?"

Noelle snorted a laugh and adjusted her cashmere scarf. "No. Please. The school hasn't done anything wrong."

"Although they do keep admitting the crazies," Tiffany said, covering her short black curls with a red cabbie hat. "And we keep inviting them into Billings."

"We didn't invite Sabine," I pointed out, shoving my hands into my pockets as a stiff wind blew by. "Cromwell put her there."

"True," Tiffany said as her phone trilled. "It's my dad. I have to take this." She moved away a few steps as Noelle, Amberly, and I started to walk across the quad. Noelle wisely maneuvered her way between Amberly and me, acting as a human buffer.

"Speaking of invitations to Billings, Reed, I'm sure you know we want you back next semester," Noelle said.

An instant thrill ran through me. "Seriously?"

"What?" Amberly blurted at the same moment.

Noelle paused and gave me a look that was half condescension, half apology. It would have been hard for anyone other than her to pull it off.

"Of course. Now that we know Sabine was behind everything, I'm sure everyone will agree," she said. "I plan to take a vote on it this afternoon, but I can't imagine who might vote nay."

At this, she turned to the side to give Amberly a pointed look. Amberly inspected her nails.

"You will accept the invitation, of course," Noelle said to me.

"Of course," I said, even though there was a twinge of trepidation inside my chest. "I mean, it will be a little strange after living there with Sabine for so long. . . ."

I took a deep breath and looked across the quad toward Billings House. My fists clenched inside my pockets.

"I can't believe I trusted her," I said, as humiliation and fury bubbled in my veins—something I clearly was going to have to get used to. I had a feeling that my relationship with Sabine would haunt me for the rest of my life. "How could I have been so stupid?"

"Hey. We all thought she was a sweet, innocent little thing," Noelle said.

"Not you. You never liked her," I pointed out.

Noelle smiled wryly and cocked her head. "Yes, but I rarely like anyone."

I actually cracked a smile at that one. Then I heard shouts in the distance and knew that reporters were firing questions at some poor soul who had just driven up to the gates.

"They're going to be all over us," I said.

"No doubt," Noelle said, staring off in the direction of the dorms and the driveway beyond. Then, slowly, she looked at me and smiled, her brown eyes bright. "Unless we're not here."

I blinked. "What do you mean?" I asked, as Tiffany finished her phone call and rejoined us.

Noelle grabbed Gage as he skulked by. He glared down at her hand, but he paused.

"What?" He looked pale, and there was a crease across his left cheek from his pillowcase. Not the coiffed Gage I knew and didn't love.

"Everyone's still going to St. Barths, right?" Noelle asked.

"That's the plan," Amberly said.

"No doubt," Gage replied, looking off into the distance. "I plan on being hammered and stupid for at least two weeks."

"So the usual, then?" Noelle joked.

"You should have a stand-up routine, Lange," Gage snapped.

Noelle turned to Tiffany. "Tiff? You in?"

"Oh, I'm so there," Tiffany replied. "Dad has a *Vogue* shoot a couple days before Christmas. I'm going to assist." Her father, Tassos, was a world-renowned fashion and entertainment photographer. "Actually, Kiran is one of the models."

Gage visibly brightened at this news. "Oh, tell me it's a swimsuit thing," he begged.

"It's a swimsuit thing," Tiffany confirmed grudgingly.

"Yes!" Gage cheered. "Hammered, stupid, *and* laid."

I rolled my eyes. Boy bounced back quickly.

Noelle focused her brown eyes on me. "Reed, you're coming with."
She lifted her iPhone and hit the screen. "I'm going to call Donnie
right now and let him know we'll be one more."

"Who's Donnie?" I asked.

"Our pilot," Noelle replied.

I laughed and placed my hand over her hand on the phone.
"Wait, wait. I can't go to St. Barths. My parents will want me home
for Christmas. Especially after all this."

Noelle looked at me as if I were a puppy who'd just peed on the
floor. "Reed. Think about it. Thomas was your boyfriend. Ariana
tried to kill you. Now Ariana's *sister* has tried to kill you. You go home,
and the entire news media is going to take over West Wackadoodle,
PA, and, while it might be *fabu* business for the local IHOP, they will
camp out on your front lawn and spend the entire break tearing into
your every secret. Do you really want to put your family and friends
through that?"

My heart pretty much stood still. I could just see the headline
now:

STALKED SCHOLARSHIP STUDENT CONFESSES: MY MOM'S A FORMER JUNKIE.

"It's settled, then. You're coming with us," Noelle said, accurately
reading my silence. "For the next two weeks it's nothing but sun, sand,
and mojitos for us." There were more shouts from the distance. The
zoom of a rushing engine. I wondered if one of the news vans was getting ready to ram through the front gate. "We can deal with whether
or not we'll have a school to come back to later," she added under her
breath.

So she wasn't that confident in Easton's staying power after all. I swallowed hard and looked around the quad at the familiar buildings and faces as Noelle made her phone call. A world without Easton? After everything I had been through, that was one blow I wasn't sure I could survive.

THE UPTON GAME

"So, Noelle, are you going to play the Upton Game this year?" Tiffany asked as we kicked back in our cushy leather seats on the Lange family's private plane the next morning. Our chairs were arranged in a sort of conversation pit, so that we could all see one another. Toward the back were four more seats, lined up against the walls like in a regular plane, except they each were singles with tables at either arm. Only one was occupied. Noelle's father, whom I hadn't met yet, had been talking intensely into his cell phone ever since we arrived at the airport and hadn't even glanced our way. Noelle's mother was already in St. Barths and would be meeting our plane when we landed.

"I'm not sure you guys could handle the competition," Noelle said, arranging the skirt of her black linen dress around her legs. She and Tiff both were already outfitted for the islands—Tiff in tan shorts, a white short-sleeve shirt, and stacked espadrilles—while I was bundled up in a wool sweater and jeans, my thick coat shoved into the overhead compartment. I was, thank God, a newly reminted Billings Girl after yesterday's successful vote, but I certainly didn't look the part. I wondered exactly how hot I'd be when I stepped off the plane.

Tiffany laughed at Noelle. "Look at the ego on this one!" She accepted a flute of champagne from the flight attendant and curled up her long legs onto her seat. I passed on my glass. No alcohol for me. Not for a while. "Come on, Noelle! It's your first Dash-less Christmas in forever. You have to play."

My heart took a nosedive that, luckily, had nothing to do with the plane doing something funky. Dash-less?

"Okay, I'm confused," I said as the flight attendant deposited a tray of chocolate-covered strawberries on the table between me and Tiffany. "A, what is the Upton Game? And B, Noelle . . . since when are you Dash-less? I thought you guys got back together."

Noelle took a long sip from her champagne glass, and then placed it down on the table at her side. "Not anymore."

I attempted to swallow. "You broke up? What happened?"

Noelle shot Tiffany a look, and Tiff focused her gaze out the window. "Honestly? It seems that once you've seen your boyfriend hook up with one of your best friends, it becomes rather hard to kiss him without thinking of where his lips have been," Noelle answered.

My face burned. I was the best friend. I had ruined Noelle's relationship with Dash. For good. "Noelle—"

"So, the Upton Game!" Noelle said loudly, brightly, slapping her hands down on her lap.

She wasn't going to talk to me about Dash. I guess I could understand that. But I felt a sting in my chest nonetheless. Our friendship
had changed, and not in a good way.

"Yes, let's fill in Reed." Tiffany reached for a chocolate-covered
strawberry and bit into it.

"Okay. Tiffany and I have been going down to St. Barths ever since
we were in strollers." Noelle paused for a moment, and I knew that she
was thinking about how she hadn't been able to go last year because of
Thomas's trial. "And we're not the only ones. There's a whole group
of us."

"Like Gage," I supplied. *Unfortunately.*

"Gage, Kiran, Paige, and Daniel Ryan, Weston Bright, the
Hathaways—"

"Poppy Simon—"

"Of Simon International," Tiffany put in, passing the tray of
strawberries to me. I selected one and took a bite. Its flavors exploded
in my mouth. Much better than the dry pretzels on my last flight. "Her
family owns this sick chain of hotels all over the world, including one
on the island. We hang out there a lot."

"Poppy is outrageous," Noelle added. "I'm interested to see what
you think of her." She leaned back and narrowed her eyes. "Who else . . .
oh, *Dash*," she said through her teeth in a tone that forbade any further
questioning. "And, of course, Upton Giles."

She shot Tiffany a sly look, and Tiffany swooned dramatically. She
fanned at her neck, opening her white collared shirt wide. "Oh, Upton
Giles . . . ," she sighed.

"You got that right."

Noelle leaned forward, and they clinked glasses.

"Who's Upton Giles?" I asked.

Noelle took a breath, swigged her champagne, and turned to us. "Upton Giles is the single hottest male specimen ever to walk the earth."

Noelle was not one for overexaggeration. If she said the guy was drop-dead, he was drop-dead. I immediately thought of Josh, who had yet to call me, text me, or e-mail me. I wondered if he knew I was headed to St. Barths. He had to have heard it through Gage or Weston or someone, right? I pulled out my iPhone to quickly check for messages. There was nothing.

My heart twinged, and I put down the phone. *Moving on, Reed, remember? You're moving on.*

I looked at Noelle. "So . . . Upton Giles is the object of the Upton Game?"

"Exactly," Noelle replied.

Tiffany cleared her throat and shifted in her seat. "Every year, all the girls in the crew compete for Upton's . . . affection," Tiffany explained.

"Back when we were twelve, it was all about who could get a peck on the cheek from Upton first," Noelle explained, slightly lowering her voice. "But now that we're older, things have gotten a bit more intense."

"Basically, whoever hooks up with Upton first wins the Upton Game," Tiffany clarified, taking a sip of champagne.

I nearly choked on a large bite of strawberry. "Omigod. Ew!" I said, covering my mouth. "You guys all have hooked up with Upton?"

"Reed! Please! I don't think my father could quite hear you," Noelle admonished, swiveling in her seat to check the back of the plane. But her father was still barking away on the phone. She settled in, smoothing her long black skirt over her legs. "*I* have not. Cheek peck back in the day? Yes. But for the last few years I've been . . . otherwise occupied, guywise."

Noelle and I avoided eye contact.

"But pretty much everyone else has hooked up with him," Tiffany added, swigging from her champagne glass again.

I looked at Tiffany. As long as I had known her, she'd never had a serious boyfriend. In a weird way, I had always thought she was sort of above the petty pursuit of guys. She usually had so much other stuff going on. Her love of photography kept her well occupied—she always was shooting for classes, for fun, for the school paper, and sometimes even for magazines in New York City. She also was a straight-A student and sang in the Easton Chorale. The thought of her with a guy was totally out of context.

"Even you?" I asked.

Tiffany blushed and shrugged. "We all have our weaknesses."

"Everyone except Taylor," Noelle amended. "She's been coming down for the last few Christmases as Kiran's guest, and she's yet to win."

"Not for lack of trying," Tiffany added, rolling her eyes.

Noelle laughed lightly, and I looked down at my hands. It was going to be so odd seeing Taylor Bell and Kiran Hayes again after more than a year. I hadn't spoken to Taylor in ages—not since the night she disappeared from Easton so mysteriously. The last time I saw Kiran was the night she confessed that she had played a role in Thomas Pearson's kidnapping. The kidnapping that had led to his murder.

Even with all of that hanging over us, I couldn't wait to see them. I suppose that time heals all wounds. Or absence makes the heart grow fonder. I guess clichés are clichés for a reason.

"So, what do you think, Reed?" Noelle asked with a smirk. "Up for a little Upton?"

"Please," I said with a scoff. "I haven't even met the guy. Besides, I'm not really into players."

Not anymore, I added silently, thinking of Thomas.

"Believe me, when you see him, you'll be in," Tiffany said, toying with the hair at the nape of her neck. She was still blushing. Whatever the allure this guy had, it was strong.

"So, what else do I need to know?" I asked, hoping to change the subject. "The Upton Game isn't all you guys do down there, is it?"

Tiffany and Noelle pretended to have to think about it. "It's the only thing *worth* doing," Tiffany joked.

"Well, there *is* Casino Night," Noelle added.

"Ah, Casino Night," Tiffany added, quickly sucking a bit of chocolate from her finger as she adjusted her position in her seat. "The Ryans throw it every year on the night after Christmas, and we all lose tons of money."

"Sounds like fun," I said wryly. "I guess I won't be participating."

"Oh, we'll front you some green," Noelle said casually, like it wasn't even a question. "You have to come. Whoever has the most chips at the end of the night wins all the money that's been spent at the tables. We usually give it to charity, but if you win, you could keep it."

My face burned. "Because I *am* a charity case."

"I didn't mean it like that," Noelle said, rolling her eyes. "I just mean, it would be great if you won."

"They have everything," Tiffany said. "Craps, roulette, blackjack, poker—"

"Poker is the most competitive," Noelle put in. "Every year the girls try to beat the boys. It's like an all-out war."

"Really? Poker's my game," I said. "I used to play with my brother and his friends."

"Nice. We have a ringer," Noelle said, lifting her glass.

"Omigod, can you teach me?" Tiffany asked, leaning forward in her seat and placing her feet on the floor. "I totally suck."

"Sure," I said. "Do you think your dad keeps cards on the plane?" I asked Noelle.

She was already out of her seat. "Are you kidding? He and his cronies take this jet all over the world. How do you think Daddy won the house in Majorca? He bluffed on a pair of sixes at fifty thousand feet."

Tiffany laughed as Noelle put her hand on my headrest. "Why don't you come with? I'll introduce you."

I bit my lip. Noelle's father was still on the phone and was obviously tense. Probably doing some big business deal. Hardly seemed like a prime time for an intro, but who was I to judge?

"Okay." I unhooked my seat belt and followed Noelle toward the back of the plane. Her father glanced over his shoulder, saw us coming, and blinked. I heard him say something into the phone about calling back, and then he flipped it shut. He stood up as we approached and tugged on the waistband of his perfectly cut trousers. He had shed his suit jacket and wore a crisp white shirt, dark-blue suspenders, and a dark-blue-and-red tie, which was still tightly knotted. He had to be at least six foot four, with broad shoulders—definitely an athlete. His brown hair was cropped close to his head in a military Caesar, and he did not look old enough to be Noelle's father. Hot uncle, maybe, but not her father.

He looked at me for a long moment before smiling at Noelle, which gave me the uncomfortable sensation that he felt I was in the way.

"Pumpkin," he said, giving Noelle a kiss.

"Daddy," she said. "You've been on the phone for so long; I haven't had a chance to introduce you to my friend."

Her tone was admonishing, and his reaction was chagrined. Was there no one Noelle couldn't intimidate?

"Daddy, this is Reed Brennan. Reed, this is Wallace Lange," Noelle said proudly.

"Reed." He cleared his throat and nodded.

"Hello," I said. There was a long moment of silence. Noelle looked at her father as if she were expecting him to say or do something.

I tried again. "Thank you so much for inviting me on vacation. It's incredibly generous of you."

"Oh, you're welcome." Then his phone vibrated on the table, and he glanced at it distractedly.

"Excuse me," he said gruffly, grabbing for the phone. "Hang on," he said into the receiver. He held the phone to his chest and looked at Noelle. "I don't really have time for social hour right now, Noelle," he said pointedly.

Noelle rolled her eyes. "Do you have a deck of cards?"

"In the cabinet."

He sat down, turned away, and began talking into the phone. Noelle stared at him for a moment, annoyed, before moving on.

"Sorry. He gets crabby when he's in business mode," she said, yanking open the cabinet. Inside were a few decks of cards, a full set of poker chips, and a folded felt poker tabletop. "Always be prepared," she said wryly. She pulled out the tabletop and chips and handed them over. We were about to return to our seats when her phone beeped. She pulled it from the pocket of her dress and rolled her eyes again.

"Dash."

My throat went dry. "He called?"

"No. Texted, the wuss," she said. "He wants to know if it's okay with me if he comes down this year. I don't know why he would, since his parents are going to be in Europe with his aunt's family until Christmas."

Um, maybe because he wants to be with you? I thought but didn't say.

She quickly texted back, her fingers flying over the touch screen.

"What are you writing back?"

"That he can do whatever he wants. I'm not his keeper." She finished her text and dropped her phone back in her pocket.

"Noelle—," I began.

"Reed," she said firmly. "We are not talking about this anymore."

"But I have to ask you something," I said, clutching the poker tabletop to my chest.

She clucked her tongue impatiently. "What?"

"If you're still mad . . . why am I here?"

Noelle thought about it a moment, then smirked. "Let's just say you're lucky I don't have to kiss *you*."

THE OFFICIAL KICKOFF

"What do you think?" Noelle asked as we stepped out onto the Spanish-tile patio at the rear of the Ryan family estate. The backyard fronted a cliff overlooking the ocean, and the water was so crystal clear I could see a school of tiny fish swimming beneath the surface. The sun shone down on the glistening infinity pool as palm trees swayed in the breeze. Gorgeous tropical flowers in bright pinks, oranges, and purples burst from flower boxes and vases everywhere. A steel drum band played a jaunty tune as waiters circulated with yummy-smelling barbecue and frothy drinks. I had shed my sweater, exposing my wrinkled T-shirt underneath, and I was still way too hot. But I couldn't have cared less.

Every stressful Dash- and Josh-related thought I'd had on the plane melted away like sorbet in the sun. One deep breath of this laid-back island atmosphere and Carefree Reed was in the house.

"I can't believe we're still on the same planet," I replied, thinking of the slush and snow back in Connecticut.

"Aw. It's so nice to see the world through the eyes of a novice traveler," Noelle said, slinging her arm around me. "Come on. Let's get some food. I'm famished."

Tiffany had broken away to find her dad, who already was there somewhere. Mr. and Mrs. Lange were standing just across the patio. Mrs. Lange had, in fact, met us at the plane, but after the briefest of hellos, she had spent the entire limo ride talking on her cell, arranging details for some fund-raiser she was throwing the first Sunday of the New Year. Now she and her husband were chatting with Amberly, her prepped-out parents, and her crunchily handsome brother, Austin, who had just arrived. I had never met Mr. Carmichael, and I couldn't help but stare at him. This man—this tall, hard-bodied, towheaded, merry-eyed man— had had an affair with Cheyenne Martin a few weeks before her death. And he hadn't even attended her funeral. Did Amberly know? Did her mother know? And more important . . . gross.

"So, where's this Upton guy?" I asked, forcing myself to look away from Mr. Carmichael.

Noelle smirked. "Let's see if you can pick him out yourself."

"Upton Game, the solitaire version?" I joked. Taking her up on the challenge, I scanned the partygoers. If I were the hottest guy ever to walk the earth, where would I be?

"Noelle! Reed!"

I recognized the squeal before I had a chance to spot where it was coming from. Suddenly Kiran's slim arm was wrapped awkwardly around my neck. Her drink spilled, splashing on my shoes, but she kept bouncing up and down as she attempted to hug Noelle and me at the same time.

"Omigod! It's *so* good to see you guys!" Kiran cried. "It totally sucks that you had to miss my birthday party, but I'm so glad you're okay!"

Partying was always priority number one with Kiran. Higher on the list than attempted murder. She pulled back and placed her now empty glass on the tray of a passing waiter.

"Let me look at you," she said, holding both my wrists. "What are you wearing? You need to get out of those New England rags and get into the islands!"

Kiran certainly had done just that. She wore nothing but a red bikini top, a tiny red bikini bottom, and a red-and-white sarong that exposed her entire leg. Her heels were at least four inches high, and the white beads around her neck were the size of grapes. Her long dark hair was swept up in a tight bun, and huge D&G sunglasses practically covered her face.

I smiled as she plucked a piece of lint from my T-shirt. Even with the fashion critique, it was good to see her.

"I told her to change on the plane, but she just wanted to get here," Noelle said with a shrug.

"Well, we can't blame her for that. Hi, Noelle," Taylor Bell said, joining us. She bit her lip and looked down at the ground before meeting my eyes. "Hey, Reed."

"Hey!" I reached over and hugged her, since she was clearly tentative about seeing me. "You look incredible."

"Thanks," Taylor said, blushing.

What little baby fat she'd been carrying around a year ago was gone and had been replaced by some serious muscle tone. Even her

face looked tauter. Gone were the rosy red cheeks, replaced by pronounced cheekbones and a slight tan. Her blond hair was as curly
as ever, but it was longer, grazing her shoulders. Her buttery locks
danced in the island breeze as she turned around to show off her
new physique and blue strapless dress.

"I've been dieting and working out like a fiend for the last nine
months," Taylor said giddily. "I am *so* winning the Upton Game this
year."

"Wait a minute. You didn't shed the poundage just for Upton,"
Noelle said incredulously.

Taylor blushed deeply. "No. Of course not. I did it for me."

But she obviously had done it for Upton. Which Noelle was clearly
about to say before we were interrupted.

"Noelle! So good to see you!"

We all turned around to find a tall girl with stunning green eyes
and gorgeous auburn curls striding toward us. She wore a green halter
dress and gold hoops and was trailed by a guy who could only be her
brother. He had the same eyes and hair color, though his was straight
and brushed aside in a preppy 'do. He wore madras shorts and a light-
yellow polo shirt, and he had a kind of tight look about him, as if he
were born with a stick up his butt. Clearly these were the Ryan twins.

"Paige. Good to see you, too," Noelle said as she hugged the girl,
though I could tell from her tone that she didn't mean it. "Hi, Daniel,"
she added to the guy.

"Noelle," he replied with a nod. "Don't suppose Dash is with you."

"Not at present, no." Noelle looked past the twins at an older couple who were now approaching. "Mr. and Mrs. Ryan. You've out-done yourselves once again."

"Ah, Noelle. Always so polite," Mrs. Ryan said.

She leaned in and gave Noelle a double-cheek air kiss, gripping Noelle's elbows as she did so. I couldn't help but notice the size of the emerald on her finger. It overlapped the two fingers on either side and was surrounded by huge diamonds. It was so big it was ugly, even though I knew it must have cost a fortune.

"Ryan family, this is my friend Reed Brennan," Noelle said, step-ping aside.

Mrs. Ryan, a Billings alum like her daughter and descended from Jessica Billings, the Billings founder, clearly recognized my name. Her green eyes quickly flicked over me, and she pushed up the sleeves of her flowing blue silk jacket, which she wore over a black top and pants. For a woman of her age, she had a seriously toned body and healthy tan, and her auburn hair was cut into a sleek, short 'do. If not for the sour look on her face, she would have been very attractive.

"Reed Brennan, the girl whose questionable leadership skills put the future of Billings at risk," she said tersely.

My jaw dropped. Paige hid a laugh and looked away. I felt myself start to close up—the unworthy Croton girl—but something inside of me said no.

"My questionable leadership skills? Do you mean the way I saved the house from being disbanded by raising five million dollars for the school?"

I'd had enough of backing down. She couldn't talk to me that way, even if this was her insanely sprawling estate. Kiran suppressed a giggle, but she didn't do a very good job. I could feel Noelle trying not to smile as well.

"Well, your insolence certainly hasn't been exaggerated," the woman said. "I can see why the girls voted you out, but I can't imagine why they let you back in."

"Calista," her husband said warningly, stepping up to grip her arms from behind. He looked at us and smiled. "Why don't you kids go grab yourselves something to eat?"

Then he forcibly turned his wife around and led her away.

"Your mother sure hasn't changed," Noelle said to Paige.

"She has this thing about speaking her mind," Paige explained.

"No problem," I replied, even though I wasn't entirely sure that was an apology.

"Ah. There's Gage. I'll catch up with you ladies later," Daniel said, quickly excusing himself.

"Never been all that comfortable around a group of females, that one," Noelle pointed out.

"Daniel? No, he just wants to catch up with the guys," Paige said, hooking her arm around Noelle's and leading us farther into the party. "So, tell me, was this girl *really* related to Ariana? Daniel says she never mentioned a half sister the entire time they were together."

Wait. Daniel dated Ariana? How could she have liked that guy *and* Thomas? They were obviously polar opposites. But then, she was a total nut job.

"Well, Ariana did have a talent for keeping secrets," Noelle said.

Kiran and Taylor fell into step with me behind Noelle and Paige. It was obvious that Paige considered herself on the same level as Noelle, which no one else in our circle would ever do. Except Ariana, of course. But again, bonkers.

A tray of barbecued chicken and pineapples on skewers passed by, and I was just reaching for it when an older couple moved aside and I saw a guy about my age standing near the railing overlooking the water. He had shaggy, light-blond hair, all combed forward toward his face and sticking out in an adorable way around his ears. He wore a black T-shirt and battered jeans and was leaning against the railing with his arms—his *very* nice arms—braced at his sides. There was a pensive look about his angular face as he stared out at the ocean. I reached out and stopped Kiran.

"Wait. Is that Upton?"

All four of them stopped, and then laughed.

"No, no, no, no, no," Paige said. "That is not Upton. That is Sawyer Hathaway."

"So very *not* Upton," Noelle added derisively.

"Although he has gotten cuter," Kiran said, looking him up and down in a pondering way as she took a sip of her drink.

Taylor glanced around, and then whacked me with the back of her hand. "*That* is Upton."

I followed her gaze across the pool, past all the glittering conversation, bleached-white smiles, and clinking glasses. It was as if time stood still. All noise ceased to be. There was no air.

Noelle had not exaggerated. Upton Giles *was* the single hottest male specimen ever to walk the earth. Tall and muscular, but in a lean and extremely sexy way, Upton had sun-kissed light-brown hair that was perfectly tousled all over. His buttery tan was shown off by his white linen shirt, which was rolled up at the sleeves and unbuttoned just enough to show off a smooth, chiseled chest. He wore a black rope necklace with some kind of ring hanging from it and had a smile that could fell a thousand supermodels. Even from across the patio, I could tell that his blue eyes matched the Caribbean Sea. He was talking to a guy with short brown hair and a decent smile, but I barely gave the guy a glance. When you were looking at Upton, he was all you could see.

Boy was hotter than Josh. Hotter than Dash. He was even hotter than Thomas. He was hotter than a grilled Josh-and-Thomas sandwich with Dash filling.

"Told you," Noelle whispered in my ear.

"Holy crap," I replied, before I could censor myself.

All the girls laughed.

"What's the joke?" Amberly asked, coming up behind me. My shoulders curled forward as all the hairs on my neck stood on end.

"Nothing you need to concern yourself with," I said flatly.

Noelle shot me an admonishing look. "We were just talking about the Upton Game."

"Oh my gosh, I am *so* in. Paige filled me in on the deets when I got here," Amberly said, the skirt of her blue flowered dress billowing out in the breeze. "And he's, like, Africa hot."

"And you're, like, five years old," I replied, mocking her voice by pitching mine up two octaves.

"God! What's your problem?" Amberly asked me.

"Do you *really* need me to explain it to you?" I replied. "I knew you were an airhead, but I didn't think you were *that* stupid."

Amberly's jaw dropped, and Noelle grabbed my arm, yanking me away from the others. "Okay, you need to chill. This is supposed to be a vacation."

"Well, it's not going to be one if I have to deal with *her* the whole time," I said through my teeth. "Do you even know what she's done to me over the past week? Talking down to me, *trashing my room* . . ."

"I'm aware, but you're going to have to let bygones be bygones," Noelle said. "Otherwise you two are going to drive me crazy. And I, for one, am here to have fun. Aren't you?"

I took a deep breath and looked around at my gorgeous surroundings. My eyes went straight to Upton. "Yes."

"Good. Now let's get back over there before they start thinking we're lesbian lovers having a spat," Noelle said.

I laughed out loud. Noelle was right. I was here to have fun. And I could avoid Amberly for the next few weeks. When I returned to the circle, I stood between Kiran and Taylor and averted my gaze from the little china doll. See? No problem.

"Everything okay?" Tiffany asked, joining us.

"Fine. We're all good," Noelle assured everyone.

"Good. Then shall we officially kick off the Upton Game?" Paige suggested.

"Wait. Poppy's not here yet," Kiran protested.

"She's not flying in until tomorrow," Taylor added.

"Her loss," Noelle said with a smirk. "By then the game could already be won."

The girls all laughed devilishly, and I rolled my eyes. This whole thing was just so silly. But they seemed to be enjoying it, so who was I to judge?

"May the best girl win," Paige said, lifting her glass.

They all reached up and clinked their glasses together. Everyone but me. Because A, I didn't have a glass, and B, I was not going to be participating.

"I'm rooting for you, Taylor," I said, as our klatch broke up.

"Thanks!" Taylor cooed, hand to her chest.

"Everyone likes an underdog," Paige snickered.

Taylor's face dropped as the girl sauntered off in Upton's direction. First impression of Paige Ryan? Ice-cold bitch. I wanted to trip her, but I didn't have the guts just then. Maybe later.

"I don't like that girl," I said under my breath.

Taylor swigged the rest of her drink. "Join the club."

"Wow. A mean word from Taylor Bell? Times have changed," I joked. A comment like that was very un-Taylor. She had always been the most doormatty of the Billings Girls.

Taylor smiled in an almost apologetic way. The wind tossed her curls in front of her face, and she casually swept them back.

"It comes from no longer having to answer to the Billings hierarchy," she said, taking a deep, cleansing breath. "You'd be surprised how freeing it is."

SINGLED OUT

An hour later I was kicked back with Noelle, Kiran, and Taylor in a set of chaise longues near the pool, my face tipped toward the sun. We were full of Caribbean barbecue and each had a piña colada (mine virgin) to sip. Noelle had insisted I change, so now I was wearing a white polo-shirt dress and a ton of SPF. My Pennsylvania skin was *so* not ready for the Caribbean sun.

"So by the fall, you'll be seeing my face everywhere," Kiran said, adjusting the brim of her wide sunhat so that her entire face was shaded. "In magazines, on billboards—"

"On the sides of buses," Noelle put in as she worked her long hair into a braid down her back.

"Hey, all exposure is good exposure," Kiran told her, raising one red fingernail.

"Tell that to Reed," Noelle said slyly.

My blood stopped cold. *Was that a jab about the Dash video?*

"The face of a whole cosmetics line," I said, ignoring Noelle's comment. "That is so incredible."

"I know. My agent said the company hasn't had a non-actress do it since, like, the nineties," Kiran replied. "I guess they just thought I was that hot."

"But not at all modest," Noelle added, flicking an unseen speck off the skirt of her dress.

A waiter in white shorts and a colorful Hawaiian-style shirt paused in front of us, smiling as he lowered a silver tray full of tarts, cookies, and slices of frosting-laden cake.

"Your dessert, ladies," he said, moving to place the tray on the table between Taylor and me.

"You're leaving that here? No. Please. Put it over there," Taylor said, flicking her hand in Noelle's direction.

"Still working on that willpower, Bell?" Noelle asked as the waiter did as was requested and moved to the next group of chairs.

"Just playing it safe," Taylor replied, glancing at the sweets as if they might jump up; hurtle over Noelle, Kiran, and me; and cram themselves down her throat.

"Understood." Noelle picked up a chunk of white cake and took a bite, then slowly, decadently, sucked the coconut icing from her fingers. I couldn't tell if she was taunting Taylor or just enjoying herself. Probably a little bit of both. "So what about you, Taylor? How's Chi-town?"

"Cold," Taylor replied. She faced forward again and looked up at the perfectly clear blue sky. "But my father bought me an entire new fall and winter wardrobe *and* a Land Rover when I told him I'd decided to stay in Chicago. Plus, I love my high school. I'm president of the senior class and should be graduating number one. Hopefully there will be an early acceptance letter from Stanford when I get home."

"Wow, Taylor. Sounds like you've got everything you wanted," I said.

When I got home, I was really going to have to deal with narrowing down which colleges I wanted to visit and apply to, something that should have been on my mind all semester and would have been if I hadn't been so distracted by Cheyenne's suicide and my stalker and my breakup and everything else. Maybe I could get a good essay out of the whole experience.

TOPIC: WHAT PERSON OR PERSONS HAS HAD THE MOST INFLUENCE ON YOUR LIFE?

ANSWER: CRAZY ARIANA OSGOOD AND HER PSYCHO SISTER SABINE.

Noelle tipped back her head and sighed. "So I guess Ariana intimidating you into leaving Easton actually was a good thing."

Taylor and Kiran exchanged a glance, and Taylor looked down at her lap.

"Is that what happened?" I asked. How long had I been dying to have this conversation?

"Basically," Taylor said, forcing a smile. "She was worried that if I stuck around, I would crack and tell the police what we did that night. Which, let's face it, I probably would have. But I never knew she went back there that night, Reed, I swear."

"I know," I replied, trying to ignore the black, festering scab inside my chest. The scab left behind by Thomas's murder, which I was now starting to realize would never fully heal. Okay, maybe I *didn't* want to have this conversation. "Let's talk about something else."

Kiran finished off her latest drink and placed the glass on the ground next to her chair. "I vote we talk about how Upton Giles somehow got even hotter this year."

She turned her gaze toward a large wood dining table shaded by a red awning, where Upton was being aggressively courted by Paige, Tiffany, and Amberly. Daniel, Gage, Weston Bright, and Sawyer and Graham Hathaway were hanging with them as well, drinking beer from little brown bottles and starting to get loud. I had to admit, Upton was fun to look at. He laughed at something Amberly said, and the laugh carried throughout the party. It was a throaty, uninhibited laugh. The kind you live to bring forth in any way you can.

He was still laughing when he turned his head and happened to look at me. My body temperature instantly skyrocketed. He narrowed his eyes inquisitively, clearly curious about the interloper in his midst, and leaned over to Gage to whisper in his ear. Gage glanced at me, smirked, and whispered back. I could only imagine what he was saying. No doubt that I was some prudish, penniless farm girl from Podunk, Pennsylvania.

Paige got up from the table and tugged Tiffany away with her, excusing herself to the bathroom. They roped Amberly into joining them as well, probably trying to prevent her from getting any alone time with Upton. It seemed there was actual strategy involved in the Upton Game.

"That's it. I'm going in," Taylor said as soon as she saw that Upton was female free. She stood up, straightened her dress, and tossed back her hair. "How do I look?"

"Very Upton worthy," Noelle said with a nod.

"You think?" Taylor was giddy. "Wish me luck."

"Luck!" we all shouted after her, earning an irritated glance, since half the party heard us. Kiran, Noelle, and I all laughed as we sat back in our seats. I hadn't felt so relaxed . . . ever. I closed my eyes and took a deep breath of the tangy Caribbean air. A girl could get used to this.

"Okay, I'm getting bored," Kiran said with a yawn. "What do you guys want to do next?"

"We need to shop," Noelle said, crossing her legs at the ankle. "Reed needs some vacationwear."

"*Bien sûr!* I am so in," Kiran said, clapping her hands.

"Ah, but you're forgetting one little problem. Reed has no money," I said.

Noelle flicked a hand. "A minor obstacle."

Yeah. For you, maybe.

"You cannot spend the entire week in jeans and a T-shirt," Kiran said. "Not with the events we have planned."

"We'll figure it out. We always do," Noelle said. She lifted her head and looked across the patio. "Uh-oh. Crash and burn."

"What?" I asked, opening my eyes.

I heard chairs scraping against the ground and looked over to

see Upton, Graham, and Sawyer all getting up from the table to follow a sullen-looking Taylor around the pool. They were headed in our
direction, and I suddenly found myself tugging down on the hem of
my dress and sitting up a bit straighter. Noelle saw my preparations
and smirked. *Great.* Now I felt like a total hypocrite. But just because
I didn't want Upton and the Hathaways to think I was a slob didn't
mean I wanted to win the Upton Game.

Not at all.

"Reed, this is Upton Giles and Sawyer and Graham Hathaway,"
Taylor said upon arrival, and not at all enthusiastically. "Guys, this is
Reed."

"Hi," they all said in unison. Upton and Graham put on bigger
smiles than Sawyer.

"May we join you?" Upton asked in a startlingly sexy British accent.
My toes actually curled at the sound of his voice.

"Sure," I said.

As the guys pulled over more lounge chairs, I widened my eyes at
Noelle. "You never said he was British!" I whispered.

"Oops." She snorted a laugh at my expense.

When I turned around again, Upton was settling into Taylor's
vacated chair, right next to mine. My cheeks turned sunburned red.
Had he overheard that?

"Graham! Come sit by me," Noelle ordered. "Let's chat."

I glanced at Kiran, who shrugged. Clearly she didn't know what that
was about either. Since Upton had appropriated her chair, Taylor was
forced to sit with Sawyer off to Upton's left. My heart was bouncing

around like a ping-pong ball. Of all these girls, he wanted to sit next to me, a milky white troll.

"So, Reed, I hear you're quite the intriguing individual," he said, sitting sideways on his lounge and leaning his thick forearms on his knees. There was a thin, white scar across his left shin. So not entirely perfect.

"Really? How so?" I asked, hoping he wasn't about to bring up the fact that I had almost been murdered . . . twice.

"Well, rumor has it you come from somewhere outside the big five, so that in and of itself is intriguing," he said with a smile. His eyes were even bluer than the ocean crashing behind us.

"The big five?"

"New York, L.A., London, Paris, Sydney," Kiran clarified. "The big five."

"Ah. Too bad for the rest of the world," I replied. "Has Rome been informed?"

Everyone chuckled at my joke, including Upton. In spite of myself, I beamed. He placed one hand on his knee, and I found myself staring at his fingers. No guy I knew had hands that large. They were not teenager hands. They were man hands. The kind of hands you couldn't help imagining running through your hair and down your back and over your skin. . . .

I was definitely starting to understand the appeal of the Upton Game.

"So, Graham, how's your dad doing?" Noelle asked.

"He's fine," Graham replied, kicking back with his legs hanging down on either side of his chair. "Busy."

"Talking to my dad, from what I overhear," Noelle said.

"What does your dad do, Graham?" I asked, mostly because it forced me to stop staring at Upton, which was starting to get embarrassing.

"He's the dean of students at Drew University," Graham replied.

"So . . . why's he talking to your dad?" Kiran asked Noelle.

"Let's just say Daddy's trying to save the Hathaway family from Jersey," Noelle replied cryptically.

"I happen to like Jersey," Sawyer said, slipping on a pair of black sunglasses.

"You would," Graham joked.

Sawyer ignored him. He pulled a tattered copy of *The Curious Incident of the Dog in the Night-time* from his back pocket and started to read, curling the front cover around the back of the book.

"Well, while I'd love to hear the rest of your opinions on Jersey, I need a drink," Upton said, rising. "Reed, would you like anything?"

Everyone basically froze. The fact that he had singled me out wasn't lost on any of us, least of all Taylor, who sunk down low in her seat.

"Noelle, pass the cake, please," Taylor said, reaching a hand out over Upton's now vacated chair. I swallowed hard as the tray was passed to Kiran, then to me. Before I could even get it to Taylor, she grabbed a nice big chocolate tart and shoved half of it into her mouth. This was not good. I was here to have fun, which meant spending time with my friends, and I couldn't exactly do that if Taylor was jealous and hating me. It was obvious that I was going to have to send Upton a clear signal.

"Actually, we were just leaving," I said, getting up and dragging Kiran with me.

"We were?"

"Yes. Noelle?" I said pointedly.

"Right." She got up and grabbed her clutch. "We *need* to go shopping. Reed was not prepared for the tropics."

"So not prepared," I agreed, rolling my eyes. "Taylor? You're coming, right?"

"Sure. Why not?" Taylor said through a mouthful of tart. "There's nothing to do around here anymore."

Noelle linked arms with Taylor and me as Kiran finished off her drink. "Boys, we'll be seeing you," she said.

"I hope so," Upton said, looking right at me.

And even though I was *so* not playing the Upton Game, I liked to think that he was watching me appreciatively from behind as we strode away.

ON THE BEACH

That night, when I came down off the high of the day's excitement—
the private jet, the natural beauty of the island, meeting Upton,
shopping with the girls—I came down hard. I felt as if someone had
emptied a vat of concrete over my head and let it harden. Exhaustion
set in around nine p.m. and the negative thoughts returned with it.
Why hadn't Josh called me? Was my relationship with Noelle ever
going to be the same? What about the rest of the Billings Girls—the
ones who had voted me out of the house? And would it even matter if Easton closed forever? As these questions crowded my mind,
all I could think about was crawling into the cushy bed in the Lange
family's guest room and passing out until morning.

Unfortunately, nine p.m. was the exact moment the guests started
to arrive at the Langes'. Of course, Noelle had to host the first no-
adults-allowed party of the vacation, thereby establishing herself as
the female in charge. And I, of course, was so not in the mood.

I heard Kiran squeal her hellos as she joined the revelers in the great room at the center of the house. Knowing that there was no way Noelle was going to let me go without a fight, I pulled on a sweatshirt and slipped down the hallway, waiting until she went into the kitchen to deal with some sort of snack food snafu. Then I slunk along the wall and out the patio doors, quickly racing down the flagstone steps to the beach.

The moment I walked out onto the sand, my phone beeped, indicating I had a text. My heart jumped into my throat, and I fumbled in my pocket for the phone. There was no doubt in my mind that the text was from Josh. It had to be. He had gone radio silent for far too long. Was Ivy okay? Had she been released from the hospital? Did he have something more to say to me about us?

But the moment I saw the message, the anticipation died. It wasn't from Josh. It was a photo message from Constance Talbot, one of my best friends at Easton. A pic of her and Kiki Rosen taken backstage the night before at this huge pop music fest called Jingle Ball, which Constance's father had some part in promoting. Their tongues were stuck out at the camera, and Chris Daughtry was in the background, looking at them like they were a couple of drunken groupies.

Which they probably were.

The caption read: YOU WISH YOU WERE HERE. I dropped the phone back into my pocket, disappointed. Why hadn't Josh contacted me yet? Didn't he want to talk to me?

I kicked off my flip-flops and stood there, digging my toes into the soft, cool sand. Taking a deep breath, I looked out at the vast, seemingly unending ocean. I listened to the crashing of the waves and waited for all the Zen sensory experiences to calm me. Waited for some kind of divine sign that everything was going to be okay.

"It's a bit intense in there, isn't it?"

I jumped at the nearness of the voice. Upton's voice. He had snuck up behind me without a sound.

"Intense?" I asked, turning around to face him. My breath caught at the sight of his utter perfection in a cable-knit white sweater and jeans. A. Mazing.

"Crazy . . . loud . . . packed out," he explained with a smile.

"I guess."

I turned back toward the ocean to prevent myself from drooling on his feet. Also because I had to absorb the fact that he had seen me leave. That he had come after me. That instead of partying with his friends on the first night of vacation, he had chosen to be alone on the beach. With me.

"Anything I can help with?" he asked, stepping up next to me.

"Help? Do I look like I need help?" I asked.

"No. Of course not. Sorry," he said with a quick laugh. "But you did look like you were having deep thoughts."

"Are deep thoughts bad where you're from?" I challenged, arching my eyebrows.

"Never," he replied. "We're very deep in England. But in St. Barths, there are no deep thoughts allowed. Did Noelle not inform you of this rule? Because if not, I should admonish her straight away."

I laughed and looked down at my bare feet. "Actually, she did say something similar."

"Good," he said with a nod, looking me up and down. "So, did you girls have fun at the shops?"

"It was okay," I replied. "I didn't buy anything."

"Because nothing could do you justice, I suppose," he joked.

I laughed so loudly I had to cover my mouth with both hands to hide my embarrassment. "Sorry, but wow. They were right about you."

Upton raised one eyebrow. "They? Intriguing. Who might *they* be and what have *they* been saying about me?"

"Just that you kind of . . . get around," I said, drawing a circle in the sand with my toe.

Upton tilted back his head and laughed. I couldn't help but grin. He had such an uninhibited laugh. The way a laugh should be.

"Well. That was blunt," he said, his blue eyes sparkling.

"Sorry, but lately I've come to believe in absolute transparency," I told him, lifting one shoulder.

"Have you now?" he asked, crossing his arms over his perfect chest.

"Believe me, if you'd seen what I've seen, you would too," I assured him.

Upton narrowed his eyes, sizing me up. "You have a dark past, don't you, Reed Brennan?"

I swallowed down a sudden lump in my throat. My eyes wandered back to the ocean. "You could say that."

"Well, then I consider it my duty to make you forget all about it," he said. "At least for tonight."

"Oh, really? And how, exactly, do you intend to do that?" I asked.

"Like this."

In one swift motion, Upton managed to sweep my legs out from under me and send me sprawling into the sand. I let out a surprised shout as my butt hit the ground.

"What the hell are you doing?" I demanded, laughing as I sat up.

"Getting you to relax," he replied.

He sat down next to me, so close our knees brushed. A warm rush of excitement crashed through me. This was it. This was when the player made his move. Part of me knew I should storm off, offended that he'd think I was this easy, but I couldn't make myself move. Then, he lay down and looked up at the sky.

"Come on. Down you go," he said, tugging on my arm.

"If you wanted me to lay down, you could have just asked," I said, moving my head around on the lumpy sand until I found a comfortable position. "You didn't have to sweep the legs."

"Right. If I had said 'lay down,' do you really think you would have?" he asked dubiously, turning his head to face me.

I blinked. "You have a point."

So when the hell was he going to try to kiss me already?

"All right then, look up," Upton said.

Okay. I guessed he wasn't. Feeling embarrassed, I did as I was told. The sky was completely jammed with so many stars that there was actually more light than darkness.

"Wow," I said breathlessly.

He smiled. "Try to think dark thoughts while looking at that."

We lay there in silence for a moment, and I started to feel calm in a way I hadn't felt in days. I let the feeling wash over me and sink in. The sounds of the party behind us—the shouting, the laughter, the music—slowly faded into a soft hum.

"When I was a boy, my mum and I used to camp out in the yard under the stars. She made up loads of stories about all the other planets and the goings-on in their unique alien societies."

"Sounds like fun," I said.

"It was. She's got a bloody fantastic imagination. Should have been a writer."

A boy who loves his mother. Cute.

"Tell me one," I demanded.

Upton laughed. "It's been ages. I'm not sure I could remember."

"Yes, you can. You wouldn't have brought it up otherwise," I teased.

Upton considered this for a moment, then he frowned. "All right, you've caught me out," he said. "I'll tell you my favorite one. It's about these tiny little creatures called Puffnicks. They live on the planet Puff."

I laughed, shimmying from side to side to get more comfortable. "Puffnicks. They sound cute."

"Oh, but they're not cute. They're actually fierce little buggers. With fangs," Upton replied. "And this story is about the year they went to war with the Bangrots."

"Oooh, I love a good Puffnick-Bangrot war story," I said, folding my hands over my stomach. "Let's hear it."

"Our story begins on one dark, stormy night in the village of Jangle, when the sole Bangrot lookout spied the mast of a vast ship on the horizon. . . ."

I sighed and settled in to listen to Upton's strange childhood story. His melodic voice was lulling, soothing, and I soon found myself drifting into the dream world he created all around us. He didn't try anything, which was intriguing. Upton was not only the hottest guy on the planet, but he was also smart. Funny. Creative. Uninhibited. And he made me forget all about Easton and Billings and Sabine and Ivy and Josh. We spent the entire night out there on the beach, telling stories and laughing, and I didn't think about my "dark past" once. By the time he walked me back up to Noelle's house, the party was winding down, and I was no longer encased in cement. Instead, I felt as though I'd been wrapped in cashmere for the past few hours.

As I made my way up to the Langes' guest room and shut the door behind me, I realized that if I had been looking for an island fling, Upton would have been perfection. But, staring out the window at the stars sparkling in the Caribbean sky, I reminded myself that I was not. No romance for me. Not for a while. Not even for Fun Island Reed. I was simply not ready.

Right?

SEXY, NOT SLUTTY

"You guys, seriously, you don't have to buy me anything," I protested as Kiran gathered up a few flowing garments in her arms. The shop they had brought me to that day was small and sunlit with floor-to-ceiling open-air windows and racks of designer clothes arranged in the center of the creaky but clean wooden floor. On the walls were displays of sunglasses, hats, and bags—all straw and thatch and woven with leather details. Upscale resort wear all the way.

After yesterday's unsuccessful shopping excursion—unsuccessful because I had refused to let them spend their money on me—Noelle, Kiran, and Taylor had insisted we go out again. And this time they were not taking no for an answer. It was consumer warfare.

"Yes, we do," Kiran said seriously. "Especially that dress."

I turned around and looked at myself in the slim mirror on the dressing room wall. The dress was lovely. Just under the bandeau top, it was tapered at the sides to show off the curve of my midriff, and then it flowed out into a floaty ankle-length skirt. It was made out of a beautiful green-and-blue silk print that perfectly evoked the ocean outside the shop's windows. I couldn't help but wonder what Upton would think of it.

Not that I was going there.

"She's right. It's perfect. Sexy, but not slutty," Noelle said as she shoved aside hanger after hanger on the round rack in the center of the store.

"Kind of like you!" Taylor added, earning a laugh from Noelle and Kiran. She handed me a little black dress with brown beading along the hem.

I glanced at the price tag on the garment and grimaced. "Honestly. I'm really not comfortable with this."

"Well, I'm not comfortable being seen with you in Old Navy all week, so just do it for me," Kiran replied.

"Ouch," I said, not really offended.

"I say these things with love," she told me. Then she took a look at my face and rolled her eyes. "Would it help if I told you I was charging it all to my agency?"

"How are you doing that?" I asked.

"I got an expense account when I landed the cosmetics gig," she said with a one-shouldered shrug. "I could be photographed at any moment, so I always have to look runway-worthy. How are they going to know these clothes are for you and not for me?"

I hesitated for a second, fingering the smooth fabric of the black dress. "You're sure?"

"I'm sure," she said. Then she forcibly turned me around and shoved me back into the dressing room with an armful of clothes. "Try the red. You look good in red." She snatched the colorful curtain closed in front of my face.

I took a deep breath and looked at my own eyes in the mirror. Sometimes when Noelle and the others insisted on buying me things, I felt like such a charity case. And I wasn't. I didn't *need* these things to survive. But I did need them to hang out with these girls. At least, that was how I felt sometimes. Like when Kiran said as much to my face, part of me wanted to walk out and just hand over all this stuff and say no. But then again, if Kiran wanted to use her expense account on me, who was I to stop her?

"Reed! Are you having a wardrobe malfunction?" Kiran called. "We want to see the next dress."

"I'll be right out," I replied. I changed into the red dress and stepped out of the dressing room.

Kiran's eyes widened, and she whistled. "Damn. Okay, not that one. You look hotter than me in that."

"Really?" I asked.

"Which is why she's definitely getting it!" Noelle put in, shoving me back inside to change again.

Fifteen minutes later, we had decided on three dresses and one top-and-skirt combo. Kiran took it all up to the register without even checking the price tags. I wondered if she had ever thought about the cost of anything in her life. Or if any of these girls had. Most likely not.

I joined Noelle and Taylor on the other side of the small boutique, where they were trying on wide-brimmed straw hats and checking themselves out in the countertop mirrors. I came up behind them and slung a gaudy pink-and-yellow scarf around my neck for fun.

"You should wear the green-and-blue to the party tonight," Taylor said, donning a pair of rhinestone-rimmed sunglasses.

"Didn't we just have a party last night?" I asked.

Noelle and Taylor exchanged a look in the mirror and laughed. "Yes, but this is the first party at the Simon Hotel," Noelle said, shedding a white hat and reaching for a black one. "Tonight, we party the way we were meant to party."

"Like rock stars?" I joked.

"Well, of course," Taylor replied, pursing her lips and tipping back her head. Then her eyes lit up. "Oh, and you'll finally get to meet Poppy!"

"Taylor *loves* Poppy," Noelle said, laying aside the hat and running her fingers through her hair.

"What's not to love? Poppy is the coolest," Taylor said enthusiastically. "We all love her."

I glanced at Noelle, who shrugged. "She's right. We do."

"Okay. That's done," Kiran said, joining us and handing me a big paper shopping bag. "Now all we need to do is find you a dress for Casino Night."

"Yeah, but there's nothing formal enough here," Noelle said, glancing around.

"More shopping?" I asked.

Kiran put her arm around my shoulders. "You say that as if it's a bad thing. If there's one thing I can teach you in this life, Reed, it's this: You can never have too much shopping."

"Hear, hear!" Taylor cheered.

"Ah, the wisdom of Kiran Hayes," Noelle joked. "You really should write a self-help book."

We laughed and were about to walk out onto the sunlit sidewalk when I saw Sawyer and Graham across the street.

"Hey, there are your friends," I said.

I noticed then that they were arguing. Sawyer's body language was very aggressive, while it was clear that Graham was trying to chill him out.

"What's that about?" I asked, curious.

I could have sworn that Noelle's brow creased for a moment in concern, but just as quickly the expression was gone. "Those two," she said fondly. "Always arguing about something." Then she grabbed my arm and tugged, forcing me to look away from the window. "Come on. You need shoes."

I rolled my eyes, but I smiled. She was right. I *did* need shoes. Heels. Nice three-inch heels that would bring me eye to eye with Upton.

Not that I was going there. Really. I wasn't.

FUN

The party that night was in the penthouse suite of the Simon Hotel, a towering structure built atop a cliff overlooking the ocean. The high-ceilinged room was decorated in an eclectic style, mixing modern furniture with a Grecian sensibility. Square couches, pillows, and ottomans dotted the room, arranged on a gleaming marble floor around ornate columns. Huge palm fronds were displayed in tall urns, and the sconces on the walls looked like colorful pieces of paper curled into cones. Weird, yes, but somehow it all worked. Possibly because no one was paying much attention to the décor. It was all about the people.

Everyone I had met since I'd arrived was there, along with about thirty other people all under twenty-one—all drinking heavily. One look at the outfits and I was grateful that Kiran and the others had forced me to shop. Colorful dresses, strappy sandals, and designer bags were the order of the day. If I had walked into this party in jeans and Chuck D's, I might have melted under the scrutiny.

I was wearing the green-and-blue dress with a pair of subtle gold sandals and a gold cuff bracelet Noelle had leant me. Kiran had put my hair up in a messy bun with plenty of wispy pieces tickling my face. I felt beautiful—and like I belonged.

I spent the first hour dancing with Kiran, Taylor, and Tiffany in the center of the room. Just letting loose and having fun. Pretending the world didn't exist. Finally the new shoes started to pinch my toes, and I had to take a break. I grabbed a glass of water from the bar and maneuvered my way to the couch, where Noelle was hanging out with West.

"So, where's this Poppy girl?" I asked, dropping down next to Noelle. Her knees were turned toward West's, and she let out a tinkling laugh as she turned toward me. I blinked. Her hand was on his chest, and he was looking adoringly at her.

Wait a second. Noelle was flirting with West? I mean, okay, he was one of the most coveted guys in the senior class with his deep brown eyes, lacrosse star body, and addiction to Ralph Lauren. But he wasn't Dash.

"Oh, she likes to make an entrance," Noelle told me. "I'm sure she'll be here soon."

I waved off a waiter offering a flute of champagne, and Noelle went back to cuddling into West's side and whispering in his ear. I couldn't wrap my brain around Noelle being with anyone other than Dash. It was just too odd. Like watching your mother flirt with the dude at the drive-through window or something. As she ran the backs of her fingers along his jaw line I had to look away . . .

. . . and ended up looking right at Upton. Of course. All night I had been trying not to search him out, and all night I had been doing just that. Right then he was leaning back against the bar, swilling a clear drink as Kiran chatted in his ear. Apparently she had decided to take a break from dancing as well, and she had gotten right back in the game. Upton nodded and pursed his lips as he swallowed, obviously tasting the sourness of the alcohol. Then he placed the glass on the bar and turned to Paige, who had just laid her hand on his opposite arm. Amberly sidled up to him as well, trying to edge out Kiran. Damn, these girls were shameless. I wondered if he knew it was a competition. My guess was no. He probably thought he was simply irresistible to all women.

Which, let's face it, he was.

In spite of myself, I slowly inspected every inch of Upton Giles. His square cheekbones. The curve of his shoulders beneath his light-blue shirt. The slightly exposed skin of his chest. He had missed a button at the bottom of his shirt, and every once in a while he would shift or make a gesture and a bit of his toned stomach would be exposed. Every time this happened, my throat caught.

I couldn't help but wonder what it would be like to kiss him. And then I realized that these girls who were flirting with him—Kiran and Paige and Tiffany—all knew what it was like to kiss him. And for the first time, that realization didn't gross me out. Instead, it pissed me off. Why should they get to win the Upton Game when they had already won in previous years? It simply wasn't fair. Someone else should get to win. Someone new.

Someone who was definitely not Amberly.

As I glanced around the dance floor, I noticed that there were couples everywhere. Graham Hathaway was dancing with a blond beauty who was at least six inches taller than him. Gage was putting the moves on some unsuspecting girl with thousands of braids hanging down her back. It seemed like every girl on the dance floor had a guy who was obviously into her.

And back home, Josh had Ivy. And I was here. Alone. On vacation. Being Carefree Reed. Screw It Reed. Fun, Fun Reed. So I was going to have a little fun. And talking to Upton would be fun. And so would wiping that perpetually smug look off Paige Ryan's face.

I stood up and crossed the room, weaving my way around the various couples. Upton caught my eye as I approached. He stood up straighter, casually shrugging off Paige's hand.

"Hey," I said, looking into his eyes.

He appeared intrigued. "Hello."

"Want to get me a drink?"

"At your service," Upton said with a half smile. He turned and signaled for the bartender.

Kiran raised her eyebrows, impressed, and tipped her glass toward me like she was welcoming me into the game. Paige backed up a touch and crossed her arms over her chest. She eyed me with obvious irritation.

"Well, well. Look who's a player," she said.

I simply smiled. My heart was pounding so hard I couldn't do anything else. Upton turned and handed me a glass of champagne. He had a new drink for himself as well.

"Perhaps we should go someplace a bit more private?" he suggested.

"Absolutely," I replied.

He took my free hand and a jolt went through me. His hand was warm and slightly rough, his grip confident and firm. Every girl in the room eyed me with envy as we wound through the crowd. My heart fluttered around on feathery little wings. I had no idea what I was doing or where this was going to go. All I knew was that this was *fun*.

Upton was staring at me.

He was staring at my profile and I was staring at the ocean, sipping champagne and trying not to crack up laughing. We were sitting, almost lying, on a double lounge chair with a thick striped cushion, on a verandah overlooking the water. The sky was this sort of purplish black, blanketed again with stars. Set against the dark turquoise blue of the water, it was like something out of a surrealist painting. I couldn't believe views like this actually existed in nature.

And I couldn't believe Upton was looking at me as if I were even more beautiful than the view. No one had ever stared at me in quite that way before. Like he was trying to memorize every inch of my face. Was this part of his playboy shtick?

The thought made me feel suddenly defensive. Like I didn't want him to think I was going into this all naive and wide-eyed like some inexperienced moron. I turned slightly on my side to face him better.

I looked into his face and managed not to blush. "So tell me . . . how many girls at this party have you hooked up with?"

Upton gave a short, incredulous laugh. "Is this your transparency thing kicking in again?" he asked.

"Maybe," I said with a grin, thrilled that he had paid attention during our last conversation.

He pushed himself up on his side and looked through the half-open glass doors that led to the penthouse. Inside, the music had been cranked up and the voices were growing louder as the drinks continued to flow.

"None," he said confidently, dropping back down. I looked at him skeptically until he smiled and added, "Tonight."

I laughed and looked away, fiddling with the skirt of my dress. "And how many girls at this party have you kissed?" I asked, my heart racing.

He reached over and simply grazed the inside of my arm with his fingertips. I thought I was going to drown in longing right there.

"None," he whispered. "Tonight."

I looked up at him, looked right into his eyes, and held my breath. I almost couldn't believe what I was about to do.

"Well then," I said. "Let me be the first."

And then I leaned in and kissed him.

How I didn't explode is beyond the laws of physics. This was pure attraction. I knew almost nothing about this guy aside from his name and the fact that every other girl at this party wanted him, and I didn't care. As he reached around my waist and pulled me to him,

I didn't care about anything other than the fact that my toes and fingers and thighs and arms and ears were tingling. I wanted to press every single inch of my body against his. Only once in my life had I felt attraction like this, and that was with Dash. And I had been drugged at the time.

But tonight, I was clear. Upton made me feel gorgeous, uninhibited, totally daring. Totally not me.

And I was loving it.

Then I felt his hand traveling from my bare stomach northward, and I jolted backward. Instantly, the crashing waves and the laughter and the music came rushing in on me. It was like waking up from a deep sleep only to enter sensory overload. Kissing was one thing. I wasn't sure I was ready to go further than that.

"What happened?" Upton asked, pulling away.

"Nothing! Nothing," I said, flipping onto my back. I tried to shove my hands into my hair, and then realized it was pinned up and carefully extricated my fingers. "I just . . . needed some air."

Upton's fingertips trailed up and down my inner forearm, sending pleasant shivers throughout my body.

"Have you gotten enough yet?" he asked, inching closer and bringing his face toward mine.

I giggled and looked at him in a mock-stern way. "I'm thinking we should go back to the party."

Upton's eyebrows rose. "Why? I'm having plenty of fun right here."

"Me too," I said, racking my brain for something I could say that wouldn't offend him and wouldn't make me sound like a complete prude. "It's just . . . I came down here to hang out with my friends, and I feel like I'm neglecting them."

Upton smiled. "All right then. We'll go inside. But I plan on continuing this at a later date."

I couldn't help but smile in response. I *definitely* wanted to hang out with him again.

Upton pulled me up off the lounge in one swift motion. As soon as we were through the doors, it was obvious that something was up. Almost everyone at the party was gathered near the front door of the suite, and there was an enthusiastic din coming from the center of the crowd. The only person who didn't appear to have any interest in what was going on was Sawyer Hathaway, who was leaning against the wall near the verandah doors, picking at his fingernails.

"It's so good to see you!" a girl's voice squealed. A girl with a British accent. "Really? Do you like it? I just had it cut."

"I *love* it," I heard Taylor say. "I've been thinking about chopping mine, too."

"Oh, you definitely should. It's so freeing!"

Finally, the girl with the accent made her way out of the crowd and into the open. She had short blond curls pushed back from her face with a skinny headband, a sun-kissed tan, and seriously defined arms. She wore a tiny spaghetti-strap boho dress with swirls of brown, red, and orange all over it, and at least half a dozen beaded necklaces of all different lengths. She linked arms with an athletic-looking girl with long black hair, tan skin, and a regal air about her.

They both giggled as they faced the partygoers, their backs to me and Upton.

"Who's that?" I asked.

"That would be Poppy," he replied with an amused look in his eye. "And it appears as if she's brought along a friend."

"Everyone, this is Sienna Marquez. Sienna, this is . . . everyone!"

"Pleased to meet you," Sienna said in a thick Spanish accent. She and Poppy both laughed as if sharing some private joke.

"Are you all enjoying the party?" Poppy asked, lifting her free arm. Dozens of skinny gold bangles jangled down to her elbow.

The crowd answered with a general cheer of approval. Daniel Ryan broke away from his friends and was about to hug her when Poppy's eyes fell on Upton. She lit up like a sparkler on the Fourth of July, dropped her friend's arm, and clapped her hands together in glee.

"*There's* my yummy boyfriend!"

I glanced at Upton, whose face broke into a smile as he released my hand and the girl came sprinting across the room. She launched herself into his arms from about three feet away, wrapping all four limbs around him like a koala and sticking her tongue so far down his throat that she must've tasted his lunch.

I was so surprised I actually stumbled aside a few paces. I found myself staring at Daniel, who was standing directly across from me, his mouth hanging slightly ajar, looking as dumbfounded as I felt. Upton had a *girlfriend*?

NOT A JERK

The next morning I woke up with a start, my heart sprinting. For a moment I had no idea where I was, and I was seized by the disturbing sensation that I was being watched. Then I saw the ocean outside my open windows and remembered. St. Barths. The Lange family's house. I was fine. I was safe. I must have had a bad dream. The sky was just starting to brighten, the darkness giving way to lighter shades of blue and gray. I listened for a moment to ascertain whether anyone in the house was up and about, but I heard nothing. No early risers in the Lange family. Not that I was surprised. Noelle had never been a morning person.

I lay back on the thick feather pillow. There was no way I was going to be able to fall back to sleep, because now I was thinking. Thinking of Sabine and Ariana and Thomas and Josh and Ivy. Lots and lots to think about.

Including Upton. Upton, Upton, Upton. My mind recalled the

image of Poppy koala-bearing him, and my chest constricted. About two seconds after that little display I had fled the party, come back here, and had gone directly to bed. There was no way I was messing around with a guy who had a girlfriend. I had learned that lesson with Dash.

Out of the corner of my eye, I saw something careening toward the window and I sat up straight, my heart in my throat. Just then a beautiful blue-and-yellow bird alighted on my windowsill and jumped from side to side, checking me out with its little black eyes.

"Hey there. You scared me," I whispered, letting out a breath.

The bird jumped back and forth, back and forth, and then started to sing. I blinked, surprised. It was almost as if he had done his assessment and decided I was worthy of a private morning concert. I was about to lay down again and listen to his song when suddenly someone stepped up to my window, scaring the breath out of me. The bird took flight with a squawk.

"Good morning," Upton said with a smile.

My hand was over my chest. "Upton! What the hell are you doing?" I whisper-shouted. My stomach was tied in frightened knots that relaxed only slightly now that I realized I knew my surprise visitor. I pulled up the blankets to cover my navy blue Easton Academy T-shirt and couldn't help wondering what my hair was doing.

But wait. I didn't care. He had a *girlfriend*.

"So this is the Langes' new house, huh?" he said, leaning on the windowsill and looking around my room. "Nicely done."

"How many windows did you pop into before you found the right one?" I asked, my heart still pounding.

"Only two. Someone should check on the housekeeper. I may have given her a stroke," Upton said.

"Upton!"

"Kidding! Kidding!" he said, lifting his hands.

I took a deep breath and silently told my pulse to calm itself. "What are you doing here?'

"I had to see you," Upton said, running his hands through his tousled hair. "You left so quickly last night that I didn't have a chance to say good night."

"I thought that was because your tongue was otherwise occupied," I said sarcastically. I rolled away from him in the bed and hung over the far side to retrieve my jeans from the floor.

"I thought Poppy might have been the cause of your sudden departure," he said with a frown. I shimmied into my jeans under the covers and swung my legs around the edge of the bed to face him. He was only about four feet away, but the wall separated us.

"Wow. You're even smarter than I thought," I said.

Upton's frown deepened. "Reed, Poppy is not my girlfriend," he said in a quiet but firm voice. "She's simply a good friend with whom I've . . . for lack of a better word . . . hooked up with a few times this past year."

"She seems to think it's more serious than that," I said, crossing my arms over my chest and glancing at the clock on the nightstand. I needed something to look at other than those deep blue eyes. Otherwise I was in danger of blindly believing everything he said.

Upton laughed in a fond way. "Well, that's just Poppy. She's used to getting what she wants—and doesn't take no for an answer. Just one of her many endearing quirks."

"Obsessive delusions are an endearing quirk in your world?" I asked.

Upton smirked. "When it's Poppy Simon, yes." He took a deep breath. "Look, she wanted something more serious and I didn't, but she's persistent. I think she believes that if she calls me her boyfriend over and over again, I'll somehow start believing it's true."

I snorted a derisive laugh. "Whatever. I just don't want to get involved in some twisted love triangle," I told him. I got up and walked over to the window. Big mistake. The closer I got to him, the higher my body temperature rose. "I'd just like to pretend that last night never happened," I lied.

Upton reached for my hand. He pressed his thumb into my palm, causing my heart to skip an alarming number of beats.

"That's not acceptable to me," he said. "I can't pretend last night never happened."

I hazarded a glance at his face. *God, those eyes. A person could die happy in those eyes.*

"Upton," I said. It came out in a sort of begging tone. I had lost all conviction.

"Just let me take you out for breakfast," he said. "I *must* prove to you I'm not a jerk."

I smiled inadvertently. His accent made everything sound so endearing.

Don't do it, Reed. Don't do it, a little voice in my mind warned. I stared at him, trying to picture a flashing neon sign in the center of his forehead that read CAUTION! GIRLFRIEND HAVER!

But I couldn't do it. Another look in those eyes and I was a goner.

"Fine," I said finally, "breakfast."

UPTON THE WISE

An hour later I met Upton on the beach, about a ten-minute walk from Noelle's house. As he saw me approach, he got on his knees and pushed up the sleeves of his navy-blue cotton sweater, exposing his perfect forearms.

"I've brought you three types of croissants," he announced. "That has to earn me some points."

He pronounced "croissants" with a flawless French accent. Could this guy be any sexier?

Do not get sucked in, I told myself, tucking my hands under my arms as I sat down on the gray flannel blanket. There was a stiff wind coming off the water, and my green hoodie was zipped up all the way to my chin, which had the added benefit of sending a clear message—not here to flirt.

"Maybe. We'll see," I said, checking out the rest of the spread. Laid out on the blanket were four separate platters heaped with fruit, croissants (butter, chocolate, and strawberry), eggs Benedict, and all manner of breads and cheeses.

"Are you a tea person or a coffee person?" he asked, holding up two silver thermoses.

"Coffee, definitely," I said, pulling my knees up under my chin.

"All Americans are," he joked, pouring some into an actual ceramic mug. I noticed that he also had somehow managed to transport a glass carafe of grapefruit juice without breaking it. As picnics went, this was pretty gourmet. Back in Croton the word "picnic" conjured images of soggy PB&Js and Minute Maid fruit punch juice boxes.

"Okay. I'll admit I'm impressed," I teased, tying back my hair in a ponytail. A few clouds had rolled in off the island side, encroaching on the sun. I hugged my sweatshirt closer to me, wondering if Upton felt the same way as Kiran did about Old Navy. I took a sip of my coffee and resolved not to care.

"Thank you," Upton said, settling in next to me with his tea. His thigh grazed mine and, even through my jeans, I felt the heat. Damn. Being near this guy was definitely dangerous. "I'm glad Noelle brought you here," he said.

"Why? Need some new meat?" I blurted.

"What does that mean?" he asked, pulling back slightly.

"Nothing. Sorry," I said, taking another sip of my coffee. "It's just . . . I like you."

Didn't get much more transparent than that.

Upton grinned. "I like you, too."

"But you're a player," I said, my heart slamming against my breast-bone.

His brow knit as he considered this. "I don't have to be."

I laughed. "Yes, you do. People don't change."

"That is such a load of bollocks. People change all the time," he protested, setting down his tea and turning toward me. "Look at Madonna. She loves the U.S., then she loves England, then she loves the U.S. again. Or politicians. They flip-flop all the time. And look at Brad Pitt. You cannot tell me that man was not a player before he met Angelina."

I laughed loudly and raised my hands. "Okay, okay! You made your point."

"Good," Upton said, settling in again. He reached for the platter of fruit and popped a grape in his mouth. "I thought I was going to have to whip out my BlackBerry and start searching Wikipedia for more examples. The point is, right here, right now, I want to be with you. No one else. Okay?"

I took a deep breath and audibly let it out. "Okay." I couldn't help but smile. He'd had me at "load of bollocks." I tore off the end of a croissant and nibbled on it. It was clearly time to move on from the player conversation.

"So what's your deal, Upton Giles?" I asked. "Where're you from? What do you do? What do you like?"

"My deal?" he said with a laugh. He propped his hands behind him and gazed out at the ocean. "Well, let's see, I grew up in Essex, where my family owns quite a bit of land. My grandfather did well with some technology investments and used his earnings to snatch up every foreclosed estate he could get his hands on, so we're new money pretending to be old." He lowered his voice as if sharing a dark family secret. "So because of this grand charade, I am supposed to make something of myself, which basically means that when I was five I knew I was going to have to graduate from Oxford and become a medic or a lawyer or a businessman of some kind. Whatever would get me quoted in the London *Times* at least once a month, which is how my father measures a person's success."

I laughed, pushing away a stray lock of hair from my face. "Sounds like a lot of pressure."

Upton grabbed a plain croissant and covered it with some sort of greenish-white cheese. "You'd think it would be, but you're missing one important detail."

"What's that?" I said.

"Expectations mean bugger all to me," he said with a grin.

I smiled and took a sip of my coffee. "What's Oxford like?"

"Why? Thinking of matriculating?" he asked, leaning on his side now. He gave me a leading look that made me shiver "We'd love to have you," he said in a jokingly husky voice.

"I think Oxford's a little out of my reach," I said, putting down the coffee and dusting some stray sand from my hands. "I'm kind of starting to stress about college. Everyone I know *has* to get into an Ivy League school, like it's going to make or break the rest of our lives. I never even thought about the Ivies until I got to Easton, and now it's, like, 'Omigod! What if I don't get in?'" I said, raising my shoulders and spreading my fingers wide.

Upton laughed and took another bite of croissant. "You don't have to go to an Ivy to have a life."

I rolled my eyes. "Said the guy who goes to Oxford."

"I'm serious," he told me. "You can get a proper education almost anywhere. It's just up to you how much work *you* want to put into it. The important thing is to go somewhere that you feel comfortable. Otherwise you'll spend all your time trying to fit in instead of trying to learn."

I stared out at the ocean. The waves were larger now, starting to splash their way up the beach toward our picnic spot. "Huh. No one's ever put it that way before."

"Not only am I not an ass, I'm also quite wise," Upton joked, spearing a piece of melon with his fork.

I sighed and pulled my knees up under my chin, hugging my shins as I looked out at the choppy water. This was an interesting concept—figure out where I'd feel comfortable. After the insane experiences I'd had at Easton, maybe I should look for a big school. Big and southern and warm. With lots and lots of sunshine, modern buildings, and no tradition at all. I laughed to myself and tightened my sweatshirt around my torso. University of Miami, here I come.

"Is it just me, or is it getting cold out here?" I asked.

My words were still hanging in the air when I felt the first raindrop.

"That's our cue," Upton said. He sat up straight and opened the picnic basket. Already a steady drizzle was starting to fall. "Leave the trays. Save as much of the food as you can."

"Just *leave* the silver trays?" I asked. Did his family sweat money or something?

"There's no time. These things come on fast," he said.

He was right. The rain was starting to fall harder, soaking through my skirt and sweatshirt. We dumped the bread, cheese, and croissants into the basket, grabbed the thermoses, and left the rest on the blanket. Upton grabbed my hand and squinted up the beach.

"We can duck under the roof at Shutters," he said, pointing at a covered deck that was mostly obscured by dozens of blossoming bushes.

Upton jogged up the beach, no easy feat in the downy sand when toting a few pounds of food in one hand and clinging to me with the other. Before I knew it, we were climbing a set of stone steps and ducking under the wooden overhang that covered an outdoor restaurant. Several of the tables were occupied, and the diners were visibly startled at our sudden arrival. The maître d' stepped forward and greeted us. He was a handsome, dark-skinned man with a huge smile and four hoop earrings in his left ear.

"Good morning, Mr. Giles," he said, placing his hands together. "Caught in the storm?"

It seemed as if everyone relaxed when they realized one of the vagabonds off the street was actually Upton Giles. I was reminded that this was a small island and that Upton's circle was even smaller.

"Afraid so, Marquis," Upton said, running his hand over his hair a few times to shed some of the rain. "Mind if we wait it out here for a bit?"

Marquis gestured with an open hand toward the front of the restaurant. "Feel free to sit in the lounge until it passes."

Upton tugged on my hand, leading me toward the lounge. But two
steps later, we nearly bumped into the Ryan family, who were walking
out to the patio. Paige, dressed in a white fleece warm-up suit, took
one look at my hand in Upton's and glanced away, irritated. Man, this
girl took the Upton Game seriously. Too bad I was winning.

"Upton! Reed!" Daniel greeted us with a warm smile. "What did
you do, go for a walk in the rain?"

"We attempted a picnic," Upton said, glancing past Daniel at his
parents. "But the weather didn't cooperate."

He dropped my hand to adjust the basket, and then left my fingers
hanging there. Paige noticed this and smirked. I tucked both hands
under my arms to feel less conspicuous.

"Why don't you join us, then?" Mr. Ryan suggested. His salt-and-
pepper hair looked as hard as a helmet, and his teeth glowed white. In
tan khakis, with his aviator sunglasses hanging out of the collar of his
blue polo, he looked like a poster boy for the Republican convention.

"I doubt they want to horn in on a family breakfast," Mrs. Ryan
said, slipping between her two progeny to step past us. "They have
better manners than that. At least Upton does," she said with a sniff,
eyeing my soggy hoodie with disgust. "Come, Paige, Daniel. Marquis
has our usual table ready."

Paige smirked at me as she followed her mother. Mrs. Ryan had
insulted me so flippantly that it took a few minutes for the words to
sink in. When they did, my jaw nearly hit the ground. Was Mrs. Ryan

really that annoyed about what had gone on at Billings this year? Having graduated from Easton at least twenty years ago, it was way past time for her to move on.

"You'll have to excuse my wife," Mr. Ryan said in a low voice. "She hasn't been sleeping well."

"Not a problem, Mr. Ryan," Upton said. "Enjoy your brunch."

Mr. Ryan flashed us his politician smile before joining his family.

"Not a problem? That woman was so rude to me," I whispered, glancing over my shoulder. Mrs. Ryan was sitting at the first table overlooking the water, staring at her menu with her lips pursed, judging the offerings just as she had judged me. "Doesn't she have better things to do with her time?"

"Don't let her ruin your day," Upton said. He nodded toward the cozy-looking lounge, filled with big armchairs and glass-topped tables. "Come on. We can get dried off inside and see if we can save any of our breakfast."

I took a deep breath. Upton was right. If I was going to be Fun Reed, I shouldn't let some bitter, bored housewife ruin my day. But I couldn't help noticing that Upton had not reached for my hand again. Was it because he didn't want Paige to report back to Poppy and tell her that he had been holding my hand? And if so, why?

I reached for a chocolate croissant and tore into it. Forget Mrs. Ryan. All these unanswered questions could *definitely* ruin my day.

GIRLS AND DRAMA

Shutters was, apparently, the go-to hangout for the St. Barths crew, as I found out when Noelle drove me and West back there that afternoon for a late lunch. The storm had been short-lived and the patio roof, which also was a shutter with slats, was open to let in the sun. Upton was spending the afternoon with his family, but Kiran already was there with her parents and Taylor, and Noelle's father had commandeered a large table overlooking the water. He was sitting with Sawyer, Graham, and a man whom I assumed was their father. The two dads were engaged in some serious conversation while Sawyer read his book and Graham texted on his BlackBerry.

Marquis led Noelle, West, and me to a prime table at the opposite corner of the patio from Mr. Lange and the Hathaway family. We were seated only for a moment when Kiran and Taylor got up to join us, bringing their iced teas with them. Kiran was wearing a demure (for her) black sundress that had a full skirt hitting just above the knee.

Taylor wore a gauzy off-the-shoulder top and white shorts, her blond curls back in a skinny headband much like the one Poppy had been wearing the night before.

"Hey, girls," Kiran said as she sat down. She started to take a sip of iced tea and then paused, looking at West. "And boy."

West grinned. He reached over and took Noelle's hand, holding it on top of the table. Kiran, Taylor, and I simply stared. Public hand-holding? I had known they were flirting, but this was big. I glanced at Kiran and Taylor. They both shrugged with their eyes, as baffled as I was.

"Where're Tiff and Amberly?" Taylor asked, sipping her tea.

"Tiff is scouting locations with Tassos, and Amberly is boycotting us," Noelle replied, pushing her frameless Kenneth Cole sunglasses up into her hair.

"Boycotting us? Why?" I asked, incredulous.

Noelle ducked her chin and looked at me. "Because of you," she said. "Apparently you're being mean to her," she added in a light voice.

I sat up straight, my jaw on the table. "I'm being mean to her? She told you that?"

Noelle's silence was confirmation.

"Unbelievable! She has been evil to me ever since she got into Billings *and* she totally trashed my room! *She* does not get to boy-cott *me*!"

Noelle lifted one shoulder and shifted in her seat, clearly amused. "Apparently, she does. And you might want to dial it down," she added, glancing pointedly at the other diners. "These are the types of people who save their shrill for behind closed doors."

My cheeks warmed, and I made an indignant noise in the back of my throat, dropping back in my chair. Who did Amberly think she was?

West chuckled and shook his head. "You girls and your drama. There should be a support group."

"Do not comment on what you do not understand," Noelle told him with a smile and a hand squeeze.

West grinned, and I exchanged looks with Kiran and Taylor again. This new relationship just did not compute. Noelle and West had known each other their entire lives and had never shown an interest before. Now we were suddenly supposed to believe they were a hand-holding couple?

"So, Noelle, what's up with your dad and the Hathaways?" Kiran asked, leaning back in an elegant pose, her legs crossed and one arm casually slung over the back of her chair. "Is he sharing stock tips or something?"

"Actually, he's trying to convince Mr. Hathaway to take the head-master job at Easton," Noelle said, closing her menu with a slap. "He has this rep for turning around troubled institutions, so Daddy and the Board think he'd be a perfect fit for Easton." She signaled for the waiter.

I looked across the patio at Mr. Hathaway. Compared to the Crom or Dean Marcus, he was so young. So . . . unintimidating. Slight of build like his sons, with jet-black hair, tan skin, and nary a wrinkle on his handsome, boyish face. Were the students of Easton really going to respond to such a man? As I looked away, my eye caught Sawyer's, and he quickly glanced back down at his book. I felt a weird rush of uncertainty. I hoped he didn't think I was *checking out his dad*. Ew.

"Where's Jen, anyway?" Taylor asked as West placed his order with the waiter. "I haven't seen her."

"Taylor! Shhh," Noelle scolded, lowering her voice as her gaze slid around to the nearby tables. "Jen Hathaway passed away last summer."

"What?" Taylor and Kiran said breathlessly.

"How?" West asked, clearly disturbed. "Why hasn't anyone said anything?"

Noelle leaned in to the table. We all did the same, knowing she was about to say something not for public consumption. "Because she—"

That was all she got out, because at that moment, Dash McCafferty walked out onto the patio. Noelle visibly paled at the sight of him, but she seemed to recover instantly. She sat up straight and pretended to be riveted by the surf crashing against the sand on the beach below. Dash found us with his eyes, and his handsome face registered about ten different emotions in as many seconds. Excitement to see Noelle. Then trepidation. Then confusion over seeing me with her. Then dread. Then recognition of Kiran and Taylor. Then, finally, shock. Because he'd finally noticed Noelle's and West's hands entwined on the table. He froze, and for a second I thought he was just going to bolt. I tensed up, deciding to rank this moment as one of the most excruciatingly uncomfortable of my life. And then, salvation came . . . in the unlikely form of Gage Coolidge. He ambled up behind Dash and slapped his hands down on Dash's broad shoulders.

"Dash, my man! You made it! We thought you were going to let the whole Brennan Sex Tape Scandal keep you away!"

Okay, so it wasn't *perfect* salvation.

Behind Gage was the rest of the crew. Poppy, Paige, Daniel, Sienna, and Amberly crowded in around Dash, all pausing to kiss him hello or to slap his hand. Before long, Marquis seated them at a table in the center of the restaurant, where they set up a loud, raucous camp. I had no idea which person's presence to focus on first. Dash, who was going to make these next couple of weeks a lot more complicated. Amberly, who had somehow gotten in with Paige and her crew in less than twenty-four hours. Or Paige and Sienna, who were basically trying to annihilate me with their glares from across the patio.

It was odd that Paige and Sienna were the ones so openly hating me, and not Poppy. Was it possible that Paige had told Sienna and not Poppy that I had hooked up with Upton before Poppy had arrived on the island? It hardly seemed possible. Girls like Paige lived to gossip, backstab, and sabotage. But then why wasn't Poppy staring me down? Did she not care? Or did she not feel threatened because her relationship with Upton was, in her mind, secure?

I let out a sigh. Maybe West was right. Maybe girls *were* addicted to drama.

"Hey, you wankers! Come over and join us!" Poppy shouted at our table, waving her hand over her head. Apparently she hadn't been clued in about Noelle and Dash's breakup. Or perhaps she was too flighty to think about it. Everyone in the restaurant smiled and shook their heads, like her behavior was just so endearing. It seemed they didn't mind Poppy's shrill in public.

"There's no room," West replied quickly. "We'll catch up with you guys later."

Poppy made a loud scoffing noise, like we were incurable losers, then turned to Daniel, who edged his chair as close to hers as it could get. He put his elbow on the armrest and leaned toward her, completely rapt with attention, as she spoke.

"Looks like Daniel isn't quite over Poppy just yet," Kiran pointed out, choosing wisely to ignore Dash's appearance on the scene.

"What do you mean?" I asked.

"Oh, Daniel and Poppy had this huge thing last Christmas," Kiran said, leaning back as our food arrived. "He was totally head over heels for her, and they spent the entire two weeks holed up in her penthouse doing God knows what. Then, on New Year's Eve, they finally came out and she dumped him in front of everyone. It was not pretty. He had one of his patented Daniel Ryan freak-outs."

West laughed and reached for the salt and pepper. "Oh, yeah. The rowboat. I forgot about that one."

"Daniel's freak-outs usually include destruction of personal property," Taylor explained, noting my confusion. "Or destruction of the face of whomever pissed him off."

"He couldn't exactly kick the crap out of the girl he loved, so he went after some poor fisherman's rowboat instead," Kiran said. "With an ax."

She used her knife to demonstrate the point before digging into her salad.

I looked around. "And you guys are friends with him?"

"I use the term lightly when it comes to Daniel," Noelle clarified, munching on some greens.

"What? Daniel's cool," West said defensively. "He just has a temper."

"Aw. So cute how you're defending your little lacrosse mentor," Noelle said, giving West a big fat kiss. From across the patio, Dash noticed and blushed, which was, I think, the point of her doing it. I was starting to wonder if there was anyone in this crowd who *wasn't* jealous of someone else, if anyone was immune to the drama.

"Speaking of lacrosse boys, I'm thinking I might hook up with Graham tonight," Kiran said, glancing over at him as she took a swig of her iced tea.

"Really? Why Graham?" Noelle asked.

Kiran's eyes sparkled. "Because he's the only one left."

"You haven't hooked up with Sawyer," West pointed out.

Kiran, Taylor, and Noelle all laughed.

"What? What's wrong with Sawyer?" I asked.

"Sawyer is the pure one," Taylor explained.

"I don't think he's ever even kissed a girl," Kiran added.

I looked over at Sawyer, who was slumped down in his chair, his book open in front of him. He wore three woven bracelets on his arm, two very tattered, the other a lot newer. "Maybe he likes guys."

"Oh, no," West said. "He's into girls. Trust me. He's just too scared to seal the deal."

"Or too polite," Taylor amended, crunching on some ice from her now empty tea glass.

Sawyer turned the page in his book and sighed, glancing out at the ocean. He didn't seem quite as stoked to be in St. Barths as the rest of us were. I wondered if he thought he was above all the partying and debauchery, or if he wished he could get involved and didn't know how. Either way, I felt for him. I knew what it was like to be an outsider in a crowd like this.

And it was never fun.

A FRIENDLY GAME

"That's you, Farm Girl!" Gage shouted as the volleyball arced in my direction.

"I know, jackass," I replied, bumping it forward toward the net.

Graham easily set the ball, and Tiffany jumped up and spiked it into the sand at Taylor's feet. Taylor barely made a play for it, then made an "oops" face and giggled in Upton's direction. Apparently she was more interested in the Upton Game than the volleyball game.

"Yes!" Tiffany and I cheered, slapping hands over our heads. Graham gave me a pat on the back as Gage whooped it up. As if he had anything to do with the point.

Dash hurled the ball under the net and it bounced along the sand, where I stopped it with my foot. I popped it up to my hands and turned my back to him, never once looking him in the eye. How the hell had I ended up on the other side of the net from the last two guys I had kissed? Two guys with seriously unresolved relationships with other girls, no less.

Answer? I was the unluckiest chick on the planet.

Of course, having Upton and Dash on the opposing team with Kiran and Taylor had one positive effect—it got my competitive juices flowing. I don't know why, but I had to beat them. Maybe to prove to them that they didn't make me nervous.

Even though they did.

"So, Upton, think you're going to win it all again at Casino Night this year?" Kiran asked, reaching up to dust some sand from his shoulder. She let her hand linger on his skin. My face, already hot from sun and exertion, burned.

"I don't know," Upton said, glancing through the net at me. "There's some new competition this year." He winked at me, and suddenly my face was burning for a whole different reason. Okay, time to move on.

"Fourteen serving twelve!" I shouted.

"Go Upton!" Paige cheered from her lounge chair.

I paused to glance over at Paige and the others, wondering if she'd purposely tried to mess me up. She was sitting between Amberly and Sienna, facing the game instead of the water. Noelle and West were lying a few feet away on a beach blanket, his arm around her back. Sawyer was sitting on his towel, T-shirt on, reading *Of Mice and Men*. I wondered why he even bothered to come along. And how many books he'd brought with him on the plane.

Luckily, Poppy was MIA, as was Daniel, so I didn't have to worry about Poppy drooling all over Upton every time he made a point.

Refocusing on the game, I tossed the ball in the air. As it came back down, I envisioned Poppy's face on it and slammed it over the net—right at Upton's head.

"Whoa!" Upton shouted. He made a last-second play for the ball, but it glanced off the side of his hand and went flying toward the rocks that lined the beach.

"Yes! That's game!" I shouted, throwing my arms in the air.

Graham hugged me and lifted me up. "Nice work!"

"Good job, loser. I'm impressed that you didn't eff it up," Gage said, reaching out to slap my hand.

"How very supportive of you, *teammate*," I said pointedly.

"Supportive like that straightjacket bathing suit you're sporting?" Gage replied. "Come on, Brennan, you gotta let the ladies *breathe*."

He mimed the universal boy sign for breasts and made some wet kissy noises. Graham cracked up, but he blushed and looked away when he saw the mortification on my face. I adjusted the strap of my one-piece black bathing suit—which was, admittedly, the only one-piece on the beach, aside from Noelle's much more sophisticated red strapless. These St. Barths girls were all about the teeny bikinis.

"Gage, you're disgusting," Tiffany said.

"Whatever, prude. You know you want me." Gage laughed, his hands on his slim hips. He actually looked annoyingly hot in his brown plaid board shorts with no shirt on. He had a tattoo of a sun on the back of his right shoulder, which was unexpected and intriguing. But not intriguing enough to give him the satisfaction of asking about it.

I felt a hand close around my wrist and turned to find Upton smiling down at me. "A kiss for the winner?" he said.

Before I could answer, he'd slipped one hand behind my neck and had pulled me in for a knee-melting kiss. By the time Upton released me, Gage and Graham were hooting and cheering and all the girls were sneering in my direction. But for once I didn't care. I'd have been jealous of me too. Because, wow, could that boy kiss.

UNHAPPY HOUR

"I say we hit the showers," Tiffany said to me a few minutes later, fanning herself with her hands. Upton, Gage, and Dash were volleying the ball back and forth over the net, and everyone else had plopped down on towels. "I am way too sweaty for comfort."

"Agreed," I said, figuring I could use a cool off, considering my knees were still shaking from kissing Upton. Waving good-bye to the others, we grabbed our beach bags and made our way up the beach toward the Simon Hotel's outer buildings. The hotel itself stood on the bluff and was accessible by a huge staircase cut into the rocks, if you were in the mood for a hike, or, if you were feeling lazy, you could get there by one of the many golf carts that zoomed between the lobby and the beach all day long. Down there were a casual breakfast and lunch restaurant and bar, a beachside pool, and a line of slim, canvas-topped huts, each of which contained a private shower.

"You really like him, don't you?" Tiffany asked as she stepped inside her own stall, closing the thick wooden door behind her. I heard her latch the lock as I walked into my own stall. "Upton, I mean. Not Dash," she clarified.

"Yeah, I kind of do," I said, raising my voice so she could hear me over the water. I stepped out of my bathing suit and slung it over the door, then added my towel and T-shirt dress cover-up so they'd be out of reach of the shower's spray. "Is that pathetic?"

"Why would it be pathetic?" she asked.

I turned on the water and leapt back as the cold jets hit my bare skin. Huddling against the far wall, I waited until I felt the stream start to warm up on my feet, and then inched my way in.

"Because you *all* like him, and he's such a major flirt," I replied. I lathered up my hair with shampoo, and then left it piled atop my head as I started to wash my skin. "Besides, he clearly has something going with Poppy."

"I wouldn't take the Poppy thing too seriously. When it comes to guys, she has the attention span of a gnat. And as for everyone else, they're just playing the game. Which, by the way, you are clearly winning," Tiffany said.

I blushed happily. "You think?"

"It's *so* obvious." The pipes squealed as she turned off the water. "I say, if you really like him, go for it."

"Are you done already?" I asked, surprised.

Tiffany laughed. "I am the queen of the thirty-second shower. Something I learned from traveling with my dad—you can never count on a foreign water heater," she joked. I could hear her moving around, getting dried off and dressed. "I'm gonna grab a snack. Want to meet at the restaurant?"

"Sure."

Her door creaked open and slammed, and I dove under the still-warm water, quickly rinsing my hair. I finished cleaning up and rinsing off and felt as if I'd actually accomplished something. Beaten the hot-water clock. And learned my first lesson of international travel. Smiling, I turned around to grab my towel.

My hand caught air. I blinked, my eyes adjusting to the relative darkness. There was nothing hanging on the door. No towel. No clothes. No bathing suit. Nothing.

"What—"

I heard a giggle and my heart dropped.

"Who's out there?" I asked.

More snickering. It had to be Paige, Amberly, and Sienna. Noelle, Kiran, and Taylor weren't about to steal my clothes. In fact, the immaturity of the stunt had Amberly Carmichael written all over it.

"Very funny, you guys. You just won the award for cleverest fifth-grade prank. Can I have my stuff back now?" I asked as the last of my shower water gurgled down the drain.

"You wish," Amberly replied, giggling.

"*You* are so going to wish you hadn't done this," I said through my teeth.

"Feeling kind of cocky for someone who's standing there in her birthday suit, Reed," Paige teased.

"And a piece of friendly advice," Poppy added, her voice firm. "Back off Upton."

"Poppy?" I said, surprised. "Where the hell did you come from?"

"I live here, remember?" she replied. "Wow. You blokes weren't kidding. She really is a stupid cow."

They all laughed and my face burned. I narrowed my eyes.

"We haven't officially met," I said loudly, talking over their giggles. "I'm Reed Brennan. Do you always treat the guests at your parents' hotel this way?"

"Only the daft ones," she replied. "Just because I've been playing nice up till now doesn't mean I haven't noticed what's been going on."

No. It just means that you're totally two-faced, putting up a good carefree, sweetie-pie show for your friends, when you're actually a complete bitch.

"Last time I checked, you and Upton were just friends," I said. "Wanting him to be your boyfriend doesn't make it true."

Poppy was silent, and I knew I had her.

"He may not be mine yet, but he will be," she finally sputtered. "Stay away from him from now on, if you know what's good for you."

My jaw dropped. I had barely even spoken two words to this girl and she was threatening me?

"Or what? You'll steal my clothes again?" I asked sarcastically, hugging my dripping body. "What could possibly be worse?"

"We'll see how you feel in about an hour," Sienna said. "Come on, girls. I'm suddenly *starving*. Let's go join the others at the restaurant."

They giggled and started walking away. My heart skipped a beat.

Everyone else had already left the beach and gone inside? That meant no one was going to be walking by here anytime soon. I was already starting to shiver. Not good. I moved my feet back and forth and jumped around a bit, trying to keep warm.

I waited and listened, hoping someone would step into the next shower or walk by on their way to the beach, but I heard nothing.

"Hello?" I called out. "Is anyone there?"

Silence, save for the waves crashing into the shore.

"Anyone! Hello! I need some help in here!" I shouted louder.

Somewhere near the pool, a reggae band started playing some happy-go-lucky tunes over some seriously cranked-up speakers. Happy hour was starting. Great. No one was going to hear me now. My heart started to pound as my skin tightened and grew colder still. How long was I going to have to stand here? What if Noelle and the others never came back to the beach? I was sure that if anyone asked about me, Paige would make up some stupid story about how I went home on my own or something. I could be standing there naked for hours.

A stiff breeze rattled my little hut, and I stepped back against the wall for warmth, hugging myself as tightly as I could. I was really starting to hate the Upton Game.

JEALOUSY

Goose bumps covered my skin. My whole body shook uncontrollably. I gritted my teeth and held my breath and tried to control it, but nothing helped. I had tied up my hair off my neck with the hair band I had kept around my wrist since I'd gotten to St. Barths, so the soaking strands were no longer hitting my shoulders. That was something, at least. But how long had I been standing there? How much longer was I going to have to wait? Every moment seemed like an hour.

And then, voices. Angry voices. Adrenaline instantly warmed me. It was Upton. Upton was shouting at someone.

". . . stupid, immature, ridiculous thing to—"

"We were just having a bit of fun," Sienna's voice replied.

My blood boiled with anger. I was going to scratch those girls' eyes out the moment I saw them.

"You should be ashamed of yourselves," Upton scolded, his voice just outside now. "Reed! Where are you?"

"Right here!" I said meekly, lifting my arm so it could be seen in the space between the top of the door and the canvas roof.

"Are you all right?" Upton asked.

A towel appeared over the door and I whipped it down, wrapping it around my shoulders. My eyes closed in ecstasy as warmth radiated over my skin.

"I'll live," I replied.

"Here are your clothes," Upton said, folding my dress and bathing suit over the door.

Oh, thank God. I quickly stepped into my dry bathing suit and yanked the T-shirt dress on over my head. They felt so warm—like they had been tumbling in a dryer for an hour—but that was probably just in contrast to the frigid temperature of my skin. I took a deep breath to calm the trembling, and I opened the door.

"I'm so sorry," Upton said immediately, pulling me into his arms. I closed my eyes and pressed my cheek against his chest. The warmth of his body chased away the last of the shivers. "They said you'd gone back to the Langes'. That you'd come down with a head-ache."

"I figured," I said, glancing over at Sienna, whose arms were crossed over her chest as she looked imperiously out at the ocean, as if she owned it. Amberly, Paige, and Poppy weren't there. I wondered how Sienna had ended up taking the blame solo, but honestly, I didn't care.

"I believe Sienna has something to say to you," Upton said, loosening his grip on me.

Sienna glanced at my angry face and rolled her eyes. "We're sorry," she said, with no sincerity whatsoever. "We were just having some fun." She offered me her hand and arched her perfectly waxed eyebrows. "Friends?"

Anger clenched my chest and I pulled away from Upton completely, stepping toward her. "You and I were never friends, and we're never going to be friends," I said, causing her face to fall. "In fact, you and your little posse can stay away from me for the rest of the trip. Far, *far* away. And I suggest, for your own sake, that you do."

Sienna's thin lips parted in indignation as I turned on my bare heel and stormed off toward the pool and the restaurant behind it. The sun was just dipping behind the hotel. I needed to find my friends and vent before I exploded.

"Reed! Wait!"

Upton caught up to me near the shallow end of the pool and grabbed my arm.

"Thanks for finding me and everything, but I really need to talk to Noelle right now," I said, wresting myself from his grasp.

"Wait. I just wanted to say I'm sorry," Upton told me, his eyes pleading. "Sienna's just being a spoiled child. She doesn't know how to handle jealousy, you see—"

"Jealousy? Wait a minute. I thought she was new here too. What's she jealous of?" I asked, a niggling feeling of ignorance gnawing at the back of my neck.

Upton bit his lip and looked away. "Yes, well . . . we kind of had a thing last term when she and Poppy came to visit me at school. . . ."

An incredulous laugh escaped my throat and I backed away from him. "Oh my God! You are a total manwhore!"

"Reed—"

"Is there any female on this planet you *haven't* had a thing with?" I asked, lifting my palms to the sky. "Maybe it would be simpler for you to list your non-hookups than your hookups."

"Reed, none of that matters," Upton said, reaching for my hands. He held them both in his and looked into my eyes. "You're the one I want to be with now. Only you. I swear it. All of that is in the past. It doesn't matter anymore."

I was amazed at how sincere he made it sound. For a second I almost believed him. And maybe a year ago I would have. But I wasn't that naive anymore. Reed Brennan had gone through some changes.

"It kind of *does* matter when I spend over an hour freezing my ass off in a dark shower stall," I told him, yanking away my hands. "This was supposed to be a fun little vacation fling. And the fun just officially ended. I have to go."

This time, when he called after me, I didn't look back.

DROPOUTS

"I should have just stuck with the original plan and stayed out of the Upton Game," I ranted to Noelle, Kiran, Taylor, and Tiffany as they followed me down the hall to the Langes' guest room, past all the indigenous pottery displayed on glass tables along the wall. "Clearly I was not cut out for this particular sport. And does he really think I believe that he's *only* into me now? After however many years of being England's number one player?"

I threw open the double doors to my room and stopped in my tracks. Noelle barreled right into me, and Kiran tripped over Taylor, knocking into the wall and taking down a potted plant. Tiffany caught the vase just before it hit the floor.

"Can you warn us when you're going to do that?" Kiran asked, straightening her top.

I couldn't respond. I was too stunned. Every inch of my room was covered in flowers. Huge pots lined the floor. Vases bursting with white and orange blooms were arranged on the bedside tables and atop the dresser. Long glass boxes overflowing with gorgeous tropical buds had overtaken the windowsills. Loose petals were strewn all over the floor and on the bed. A handwritten note sat propped up on my pillow.

"My mother is so going to fire Maritza when she sees this mess," Noelle said, nudging some petals with her foot. "Dammit. There goes her good espresso!"

"Who're they from?" Taylor asked, her eyes bright.

My first thought was of Josh. Had Josh talked to Ivy and explained that he still loved me? My heart beat wildly with curiosity as I picked up the card, not daring to imagine what it might say. The handwriting was unfamiliar, and my eyes went directly to the signature. I forced a smile. "They're from Upton," I said, silently scolding myself for letting my thoughts turn to Josh. That was over. I was moving on. And clearly Upton was more than willing to help me speed up the process.

"How did he pull this off?" Tiffany asked, lowering her nose to the nearest arrangement. "We just left him. Does he have the florist on speed dial?"

"Dear Reed," I read. "Please accept these flowers as my sincere apology. I promise that tonight, you will have my full and undivided attention, if you so choose to allow it. Love, Upton." My heart fluttered.

"Wow. He really likes you," Taylor said, fingering the soft petals of a huge white lily. She took a deep breath and let her hands slap against her thighs. "Well, that's it. I'm officially dropping out of the Upton Game."

"Really?" I said.

"What's the point?" Taylor asked, lifting her arms to take in the entire room. "You have his full and undivided attention."

Kiran sighed audibly. She took a lipstick out of her clutch and leaned toward the mirror on the dressing table. "Guess it's Graham Hathaway for me."

"Poor guy has no idea what he's in for," Noelle joked.

"No, he does not," Kiran agreed, pressing her lips together.

The flutter in my heart took on a whole new excited rhythm. My competitive side couldn't help but feel a bit proud. Apparently I had won. Upton, the most coveted and sought-after guy in their group, was all but mine.

Unless, of course, Poppy had anything to say about it.

But in the past few hours, I had taken Tiffany, Kiran, *and* Taylor out of the game. Three very worthy contenders. If I could intimidate them, I could intimidate anyone. Even Poppy Simon.

Suddenly, I couldn't wait until tonight.

YIN AND YANG

Upton wasn't kidding. All night he danced with me, sat down with me when I needed a break, ran to get me drinks the second I mentioned I was thirsty, and got me chips to munch on when I was hungry. All night I ignored the hostile stares of Sienna and Amberly and Paige. It was like I was Cinderella, and they were the ugly stepsisters watching me steal the prince's attention. It was perfect. But not just because I had won some stupid game. That felt good, of course. But it wasn't about that. It was about Upton. Me and Upton. It was as if we were in our own little world where no one else could touch us.

That is, until Poppy arrived.

Upton and I were on the outskirts of the dance floor—basically a lacquer platform set atop the sand and surrounded by pillow-topped benches—when Poppy walked in, turning heads. She wore nothing but a skimpy white bathing suit under a see-through gauze mini-skirt, and the thin woven straps of her heeled sandals wound all the way up her toned calves. Her first stop was at the DJ booth, where she whispered something to the shirtless spinner, then grabbed his microphone.

"Where're my girls?" she shouted at the top of her lungs, throwing her arm in the air. Sienna, Paige, Amberly, Kiran, Taylor, Noelle, and Tiffany—all of whom were in the center of the dance floor—hollered in response, throwing their arms up as well. "Ladies! It's time we show the rest of these slags how to party!"

Poppy jumped down from the DJ booth and danced her way through the crowd, pressing up against every hot guy as she made her way over to her friends. Girls danced with her, and guys eyed her apprecia- tively. Clearly Poppy knew everyone on this island, and everyone was stoked to see her. Everyone but me.

"Noelle wasn't kidding. Poppy definitely knows how to make an entrance," I said. My black minidress suddenly felt like a garbage bag in comparison to her outfit.

Upton glanced over his shoulder at her. "Yes, but we don't care about her, remember?"

Perfect response. My heart turned to goo. I grinned and reached up to wrap my arms around his neck. "Oh, I remember."

Upton smiled and gave me a questioning glance, as if he were afraid to misread the obvious signal I was broadcasting:

Kiss me! Kiss me! Kiss me!

Then he finally leaned in and touched his lips to mine. Every one of my limbs went limp, and I momentarily forgot where I was. Nor- mally I'm not one for huge, prolonged public displays of affection, but we stood there on the dance floor and just kissed for a long, *long* time.

When Upton finally broke away, he kept his arms wound tightly around me. "I've been thinking about that all night."

"Me too," I said, resting my cheek on his chest and sighing happily.

So not caring about Poppy. So not caring . . .

But it was total crap. Of course I cared about her. I cast a sidelong glance in Poppy's direction and saw that, sure enough, Sienna was whispering in her ear and glancing pointedly at Upton and me. Poppy's eyes narrowed as she spotted us.

Adrenaline filled my veins, bubbling hot as lava. I held Upton tighter as we danced. Two seconds later, I felt a sharp finger jabbing repeatedly into my back.

"Excuse me."

I checked Upton's face before I turned around. He looked rather ill. Not a good sign. I steeled myself and faced Poppy.

"Yes?" I said.

"I thought we had an understanding," she said, with a smile that didn't reach her eyes. "Or were you not paying attention?"

"Oh, I got the message," I said coolly. "I just chose to ignore it."

Then I turned my back on her and reached for Upton. Her hand gripped my shoulder, her bony fingers digging into my skin.

"May I cut in?" she asked through her teeth.

The music pounded inside my head as I waited for Upton to say something. Anything. I waited a good sixteen bars. Upton just stood

there behind me, silent, while my body temperature climbed steadily
with each driving beat.

"Is she deaf or just slow?" Poppy joked, glancing past me toward
her "boyfriend." "I said, may. I. Cut. In?"

"I don't know," I replied. "It's up to Upton."

I looked into his eyes. It was now or never. Time to see what the
Up-man was made of. If he blew me off, I would walk away. Even
though I *so* didn't want to walk away.

Upton took a deep breath and sighed, looking at the ground and
scratching his eyebrow with his index finger before facing her.

"Poppy, we need to talk," he began.

He took her hand and walked her off the dance floor, just a few feet
away from where we'd been standing. Unsure of what to do, I glanced
around and saw Daniel exchange an interested glance with Paige.
They both made their way over, hanging back a respectable distance,
but definitely within eavesdropping range. Soon enough, most of the
crew was gathered in the same way, pretending not to be listening in.
Pretending quite badly.

"What is it, poodle?" Poppy asked, putting her arms around his
waist.

Upton took her wrists and placed them back at her sides. She
blinked, obviously upset, and glanced around. She noticed a few
people watching and lifted her chin, trying to mask her surprise.

"This has to stop," Upton said, firmly but not unkindly. "I'm
sorry, but I don't know how much clearer I can be. We've never
been together—and we never *will* be together. We're friends. And

as your friend, I'm telling you to stop embarrassing yourself."

Poppy took a step backward, heartbreak written all over her face. A few girls nearby laughed behind their hands. Poppy looked at them, confused. Clearly she was not accustomed to being the object of laughter. I glanced over at Noelle and the others, and every last one of them looked like they wanted to flee. Like they'd rather be doing anything other than witnessing this. Which I supposed I understood. It was even hard for me to watch, and they actually were friends with Poppy. No one liked to see their friend get dissed.

"Is this because of her?" Poppy asked.

"Not entirely, no," Upton said, putting his hands in his pockets. "I just don't feel that way about you. I'm sorry."

Paige and Sienna stepped forward, but Poppy whirled around, searching the club for someone.

Oh, crap. Me.

The girl crossed the few feet between us in about half a second, knocking over an oblivious partier in the process, sending her margarita flying. Poppy got so up in my face that I could count the pores on her nose. My heart pounded with trepidation, and I could only hope it didn't show on my face.

Never let your rival see you sweat.

"I've been meaning to ask you. How does it feel to be a one-person natural disaster?" Poppy spat. Literally spat. Her saliva pelted me just below my left eye.

"What are you talking about?" I replied, quickly wiping away the spittle.

"You! Hurricane Reed. You leave a wake of destruction every-where you go," she said, crossing her arms over her chest. "Broken relationships, crushed hearts . . . death."

Tears stung my eyes as I stared back at her. I so wanted to be unruf-fled by her attack, but how could anyone remain unaffected in the face of that sort of characterization? Was this actually what people were saying about me? Was this really what people thought? Every inch of my skin burned with anger, humiliation, and hurt.

"Don't think I don't know what happened to Thomas, to that girl in your dorm," she went on. "People talk—and somehow, they always talk about *you*. You're dangerous."

I was so stunned, I didn't know how to respond.

"Poppy. That's enough," Upton said, coming up behind her.

"Screw you," she said, whirling on him. "Screw the both of you. Good luck trying to survive the storm."

Then she turned and ran out of the club. Daniel tried to follow, but she was too quick. She hopped in her white BMW and peeled away so fast that she almost spun out and crashed into a sand dune. Everyone in the place gasped, but she managed to back up and race off. Her tail-lights disappeared around a bend, and the crowd slowly returned to its partying. I simply stood there, staring after her. No one had ever said anything that cruel outright to me. I couldn't keep her words from repeating themselves in my mind.

Wake of destruction . . . one-person natural disaster . . . crushed hearts . . . death . . . Part of me felt the truth of it all. I was a huge sucking funnel cloud of bad luck, bringing misery to everyone I knew.

Thomas, Cheyenne, Ivy, Josh, Dash, Noelle. Even Taylor and Kiran still would be enrolled at Easton if I had never shown up there. No one was safe from Hurricane Reed.

"Well, that was fairly intense," Upton said, reaching for my hand. "Are you all right?"

"No. Not really," I replied, my voice trembling.

"Hey. Don't listen to her," Upton said, tipping up my face with his finger. "That's just Poppy. When she's upset, she feels the need to tear down everyone around her. And she's always been quite skilled at it."

A breeze caught my hair, and I shivered violently. I could only imagine how Poppy was going to treat me for the rest of our vacation. At the very least I was sure I was in for a lot of glares and behind-my-back whispers. But if she was anything like the rest of her friends, I also could look forward to a lot more childish pranks like the shower fiasco—probably worse. Was anyone, even Upton, worth all that?

And did he really want to stand directly in the storm path of Hurricane Reed?

"She's right, though," I said, pulling away from him and hugging myself. "You should stay away from me. Every time anyone gets close to me . . . something bad happens."

Upton smirked. "Well, that's a risk I'm just going to have to take," he said, stepping closer and reaching out to tuck my hair behind my ear. He let his fingers linger on my cheekbone as he looked into my eyes. "You still don't get it, do you? You've done something to me, Reed Brennan. I can't seem to stop thinking about you." He took a deep breath and gazed out at the ocean. "It's bloody annoying, actually."

He cracked a smile and I couldn't help it. I smiled back. Okay, so maybe he was worth it. There was something about being with Upton that made it difficult to stay in a negative frame of mind. Jealousy, apprehension, sadness, self-pity—they all seemed to flit away when he was near. When it came down to it, it seemed that he was exactly what I needed. The light and happy yang to my seriously depressing yin.

"Sorry. I hate to be an annoyance," I joked in return.

He pulled me into a hug, the warmth of his arms instantly chasing away the chill, and rested his chin atop my head.

"I will only consider you an annoyance if you refuse to dance with me right now," he replied as the DJ switched over to a slow tune.

"I suppose I could oblige," I said with a grin.

Upton tugged on my fingers, and I followed him back onto the dance floor. I could still feel Paige, Sienna, and the others watching us, but I concentrated on Upton, making sure I didn't give any of them the satisfaction of catching their eyes. Wrapped safely in Upton's arms, I shut out all the angry, curious, jealous stares. As we swayed back and forth to the music, I let it all go, simply listening to his breathing and feeling the rise and fall of his chest.

Despite everything else that had happened, that moment, at least, was perfect.

FACE-TO-FACE

In the end, Upton did not spend every single second of the night pinned to my side. After all, sometimes a guy has to pee. It was at one such solo moment that the encounter I had been dreading finally happened. I was standing at the bar, waiting for a glass of ice water, when I saw a familiar hand next to mine. Just seeing those fingers brought back flashes of memories I didn't want to recall. Bare skin, zippers undone . . .

Hands . . . everywhere.

"Dash."

"Hey, Reed."

My heart was in my throat as the bartender placed my glass in front of me. I picked it up and tried to turn the other way. Away from him. But he touched my forearm lightly.

"Don't. Please."

Damn. Damn him and his politeness.

I took a deep breath and held it for strength, then turned and forced myself to look at him. To really look into his warm brown eyes. They were totally miserable.

"Sorry," he said, releasing me and shoving his hands into the pockets of his pressed chinos. Over them, he wore a white T-shirt and a blue-and-yellow Canterbury rugby sweater. The uberpreppy look so worked for Dash. Worked so well that every other girl in our vicinity was eyeing him hungrily as they sipped their drinks. Not that he would ever notice. "Sorry. I just . . . how are you?" he said.

"Fine," I replied.

"I heard about everything. What happened the night of Kiran's party . . . ," he said. "I was . . . worried."

"Look, Dash, I really don't think we should be talking to each other," I said, glancing around warily. Noelle may have been pretending to be over Dash, but I knew she was anything but. And I also knew what images would be conjured if she saw the two of us together.

"I don't care about that right now," he said firmly. "There's something I have to say to you. It's been way too long."

I took another breath. *Where was this going? Please don't let him be about to profess his undying love, because I really don't think I can deal with that just now.* Although it would have been flattering. He was, after all, Dash McCafferty.

"Did you ever get that e-mail?" he asked, running his fingers along the edge of the black lacquer bar top.

I blinked. For a moment I had no idea what he was talking about. I thought back, back to all the drama, all the conversations and unanswered questions, and a lightbulb suddenly went off in my mind. The e-mail. He'd sent it to me after the Legacy incident, and I'd been about to read it when I'd noticed there were hundreds of e-mails from Cheyenne's ghost in my in-box. Well, from Sabine, really. But at the time, I hadn't known that. Freaked, I had shut down my computer.

"No. I never read it," I told him.

Dash blew out a sigh. "I guess it's better face-to-face anyway." He looked at me and put his hand, palm up, on the bar. "I just wanted to apologize," he said. "For that night. For what happened at the Legacy. I was totally out of line. I had already decided to get back together with Noelle, but when I got that note from you—"

"Wait. You got a note from me?" I blurted.

Dash blinked. "Um . . . yeah." He said it like, "Um . . . *duh!*"

"Omigod," I said, closing my eyes and resting my glass on the bar. I had to take a deep breath. Sabine's plan had been even more intricate than I'd realized.

"Anyway, I was so curious," Dash continued. "And then when I saw you . . . I don't know what happened. I mean, it's not that I wasn't attracted to you . . . we both know I was . . . but I—" He stopped, frustrated by his own lack of focus. "It's just, that was so not me. I don't cheat. Ever."

I stared at him for a long moment. He didn't know. No one had told him. I had figured that Gage or someone would have relayed everything Sabine had said the night of the shooting. All of her confessions. But clearly they hadn't thought it was important enough. Guys. When it came to dissemination of gossip, they were sorely lacking.

"Dash, I know it wasn't you," I said. "It was Sabine. She did all of it."

Dash's brow creased. "What do you mean?"

"She sent us the notes. She laced our drinks with ecstasy. She basically orchestrated the whole thing," I told him. "She confessed to all of it the night she shot Ivy."

Dash sort of froze. He looked like a cardboard cutout of himself, eternally posed in an expression of shock. Then, finally, he bent at the waist and sat down on the vacant barstool behind him.

"Oh my God. I was drugged?" he said.

I nodded. "We both were," I confirmed. "It wasn't our faults."

Then I blushed, thinking back to our almost-kiss in Martha's Vineyard last summer, all the flirtatious e-mails we'd written, the moment we shared at the Driscoll Hotel last fall. All the things that had led up to that night.

"Well, not entirely our faults," I amended, bringing a blush to Dash's cheeks as well.

"I knew it. I *knew* something was off that night." He turned toward the bar and brought his hand to his mouth, chewing on his thumbnail for a moment. "And Noelle knows all this?"

"She does," I said.

Dash's jaw clenched. I could practically feel him trying to contain his emotions. "Then I guess she really is done with me," he said. "If she knows all this and she's still with West."

I somehow managed to contain a laugh. He couldn't actually think she was *with* West in any real way. He couldn't be *that* clueless. But then, he was a guy in love. I suppose that could account for a tiny slip in the IQ. I didn't want to tell him about my firmly held belief that Noelle was only smooching West to make Dash jealous. Noelle was, after all, my friend. But I had to say something, if only to wipe that pathetic look off of his normally confident face. Besides, I was sure that Dash was the person Noelle wanted to be with. If I could facilitate their reunion and get things back to normal, all of us would be a lot happier.

Except West. But you can't please everyone.

"I don't think they're serious," I hedged.

"No?" he asked hopefully, his shoulders straightening.

"Nah. Probably just an island fling," I said. "Don't give up yet."

Dash chuckled. "Thanks, Reed." He spun on the bar stool to face me, and then stood up. "So . . . friends?"

Friends. It was what we always had been. How we should have remained all along.

"Friends," I replied with a nod.

MISSING

The next morning I awoke to the song of my feisty island bird. I opened my eyes and there he was, hopping around on the windowsill. I smiled, let out a yawn, and stretched.

"You're back," I said quietly.

He jumped around in a circle as he sang. Like, *What? You thought I was going to desert you?*

I rolled onto my back and smiled, listening to his song and recalling all the perfect moments from the night before. After my talk with Dash, Upton and I had taken a walk along the beach, kicking water at each other and trying to tackle each other into the waves. He had driven me home and had walked me to the front door for a goodnight kiss.

My heart fluttered at the memory. I scooted down in my bed, pulling the soft white sheets up over my head and letting out a little squeal. I hadn't entertained many expectations coming into this trip.

I figured I'd read a few books on the beach, maybe get a tan, do the club thing with Noelle. But I hadn't thought beyond that, and I certainly never expected this. I never expected to meet someone and to feel this way. Like I was falling in—

My rogue thought was cut off by the sound of frantic pounding. The bird took off with a startled jolt, and I sat up straight, tossing off my sheets. Someone was at the front door of the house. I heard Noelle's father say something to one of the servants, and another door in the house slammed.

Should I go check out the commotion, or should I let the family deal with it? This was their house, their island, their friends. Maybe I would just be interfering. I hesitated behind my closed bedroom door until my curiosity got the better of me. Then I tiptoed down the hall to the open foyer, thinking I could sneak back to my room if I didn't want to get involved.

Noelle was meeting her father at the door. He was already dressed in creased khakis and a button-down shirt. She was wearing a black silk robe over a black silk nightgown. I looked down at my boxer shorts and rumpled gray Penn State T-shirt. Maybe it was time to invest in some grown-up night clothes.

I also couldn't help but notice that a fat Christmas tree had appeared in the middle of the great room, as if from nowhere, decorated from top to bottom with silver and white balls, bells, and thick silver ribbon for garland. Evergreen swags hung on the walls, centered by silver bows, and silver-and-white fur stockings were tacked along the breakfast bar. There even was one with my name sewn into it. None of this had been there when we went to bed the night before. Did the Langes have a fleet of Caribbean elves working for them?

"I've got it," Mr. Lange said to Noelle, reaching for the door.

Paige and Sienna stood on the doorstep in casual gear: shorts and tank tops, with matching oversized Chanel quilted bags— Paige's green, Sienna's red. They both froze at the sight of Noelle's father.

"Girls?" he said.

Paige pushed up her huge sunglasses on top of her head. "We're so sorry to bother you, Mr. Lange, it's just . . . Poppy is missing."

"What?" Noelle and her father said in unison. He took a step back. "Please, come in."

They walked into the foyer, but no one made a move toward the living room. Paige spotted me, and instantly her expression turned disgusted, as if she'd just sucked on a lemon. I stepped into the room. There would be no sneaking away now.

"What do you mean, missing?" Noelle demanded, retying the belt on her robe.

"I went over there this morning to bring her the standard post-breakup, you-can-do-better-than-him breakfast, and she wasn't in her room," Paige began. She gave me another loathing look, as if to remind me of my role in last night's dumping.

"Her bed hadn't been slept in," Sienna added in her thick accent, hitching her purse higher on her shoulder.

"So she never came back to the suite last night?" Noelle asked Sienna.

"No. But the suite is so huge . . . I hear nothing from her side of the room when she *is* there," Sienna replied.

"So we were walking around the hotel grounds looking for her, when one of the workers came running into the lobby all freaking out," Paige continued. "They found Poppy's car down by the family's private dock with the driver's side door open—and there was blood on the ground."

"Oh my God," I heard myself say. My hand automatically flew to my mouth.

"The Simons' thirty-footer is gone," Sienna added. She had yet to even look at me or in any way acknowledge that I was there. "We tried to find her parents, but the hotel people told us they're visiting friends in Antigua for the next two days."

"And their cell phones went straight to voice mail," Paige added.

My hands were slick with sweat. Missing? Blood? We had come to St. Barths to put a situation like this one behind us. Poppy's words from the night before suddenly started to echo in my mind.

Path of destruction . . . crushed hearts . . . death . . . .

Maybe she was right. Maybe it really was me. Maybe I brought misery everywhere I went.

"What should we do?" Paige asked, looking at Mr. Lange. "What if someone kidnapped her and stole the boat, and she's out on the open sea with some psycho?"

Noelle snorted a laugh, and Paige looked at her like she had just thrown up on her Jimmy Choos.

"This isn't funny," she snapped.

"Now, girls. You don't know that something bad has happened to her," Mr. Lange said in a comforting tone.

"Exactly," Noelle added, throwing out her hands. "This is Poppy we're talking about. The girl who once disappeared from her boarding school for an entire semester to go hot air ballooning over Austria and didn't bother to tell anyone."

Hot air ballooning? Cool.

"But what about the blood?" Paige asked. "Explain that."

"Maybe she tripped on those ridiculous shoes she was wearing and cut open her knee," Noelle suggested. "I just think it's too soon to panic, that's all."

It was amazing how Noelle's rationalization calmed me. Perhaps it was because she had turned out to be right so many times in the past. But suddenly, the visions of me as some kind of magnet for evil melted away. If Noelle thought Poppy was fine, then she probably was.

Just then, there was a rap on the still-open front door. We all turned to find Upton loitering on the doorstep in jeans and a light-blue shirt, looking like he'd just stepped out of a cologne ad. My heart skipped a beat. Paige and Sienna both lit up briefly at the sight of him, but then Sienna glowered and looked away. It seemed that, for a moment, the sight of his beauty had made her forget she was mad at him.

"Upton," Paige said, touching her perfect hair.

My hands flew to the rat's nest atop my own head. I quickly tied it back, and then crossed my arms over my chest, which was bra-free.

Had I washed my face last night, or did I have raccoon-style mascara smudges under my eyes? God, Reed, when were you going to learn? You never know when a guy is going to show up without notice. Thomas, Josh, and now Upton. It was one thing these guys had in common, it seemed. They were all fans of the drop-by.

"Good morning," Upton said cheerfully, coming into the house and glancing around at our circle. "Noelle, are you having a breakfast party and didn't invite me?"

Sienna whirled on Upton. "This is your fault!" she said, shoving his shoulder.

He was so startled that he actually tripped back a step. "Hold on a sec," he said, raising his palms. "What did I do?"

"Apparently, Poppy is missing," Noelle explained. "Her car was deserted, there was blood, and the *Simon Says* is missing from its slip."

Simon Says? That was the boat's name? How . . . cutesy.

Upton laughed. "Please. She's not missing. She's just out for a sail."

Paige threw her hands up. "Why are we the only people who are concerned about this?"

"Paige, this is what Poppy does," Upton said. He reached out and put his hand on her bare shoulder, which made her blush all the way up her neck and into her face. "She's probably gone off to some private island to meditate with a shaman or something. Tonight we'll all meet up at the hotel, and she'll be sitting at the bar waiting to tell us all about it."

"Hijo de puta," Sienna said through her teeth.

Upton's eyes widened. "Pardon me?"

"You broke her heart! She ran off upset!" Sienna ranted. "You know what she is like when she is in that mood. Who knows what she could have done, or with whom? If anything happens to her, Upton, it's your fault."

She pushed past him and disappeared through the door. Paige glanced around at us, looking stunned and slightly embarrassed by Sienna's breakdown.

"I guess that's my cue," Paige said. She paused as she stepped past Upton, looking him up and down suspiciously. "What are you doing here, anyway?"

Upton took a deep breath and let it out audibly, as if shaking off Sienna's attack. "Well, I've come to take Reed horseback riding, if she's interested," he said, flashing a smile in my direction.

Both Mr. Lange and Noelle looked at me curiously. I wondered what Mr. Lange was thinking. He wasn't going to tell me I couldn't go, was he? Pull a concerned chaperone or surrogate father move? But he just looked away when he saw me watching him, and he said nothing.

"I don't know. Did we have anything planned for today?" I asked Noelle.

"Yes. I have a plan to go back to sleep," she said. "Feel free to ride all the horses you want."

"Okay. I guess I'll go get ready," I said giddily.

"And Paige, I'll keep trying Poppy's parents," Noelle's father said. "I'm sure they'll have some explanation."

"Thanks, Mr. Lange," Paige said with a smile. She eyed me, Upton, and Noelle in a scolding manner. "At least someone around here cares."

Then she slid her sunglasses over her eyes, turned, and walked off with her chin in the air.

"Like she actually cares about anyone other than herself and her mentally twisted brother," Noelle said, rolling her eyes. "I'll see you guys at Shutters for brunch. *Late* brunch." She strolled off toward her room.

"Give me ten minutes," I told Upton.

"I'll give you fifteen, even," he replied with a grin.

"Tea, Upton?" Noelle's father offered.

"Sounds perfect."

The two of them went off toward Mr. Lange's office near the back of the house, and I could have sworn I heard my name mentioned. But I had more important things to consider than what was probably a polite conversation about how Upton and I had gotten together. Like what, exactly, did a girl on an exclusive Caribbean island wear to go horseback riding?

FLING FLUNG

"Um, what are we doing on Paige's estate?" I asked, sitting on a bale of hay inside the Ryans' state-of-the-art stable as Upton hoisted up a saddle on a beautiful gray mare. At least I assumed it was state-of-the-art. I'd never actually been in a stable before. But with automated doors on the dozen stalls; a stainless steel scrubbing area; and shelves of gleaming saddles, bridles, and brushes, it sure seemed well appointed. None of it had held my attention for very long, however, because Upton was fairly mesmerizing. He had shed the shirt soon after our arrival and was now wearing nothing but a tight white tank top over his jeans. Watching him move around the stable, all self-assured and half-dressed, was making my head fuzzy and my skin tingly and warm.

"They're the only ones on the island with enough property to keep horses, so we board our animals here," he said, reaching under the horse's belly for one of the straps. He buckled it tightly, then came around to my side and slapped the horse's back. "This one's Misty. I've had her since I was fourteen, and I promise she'll treat you well."

"Unlike all your other women," I joked, pushing myself up and dusting my hands off on the butt of my jeans.

"Haven't we gone over this? I have no other women," Upton said fondly, handing me a bucket full of carrots. "Here. Feed her a couple of these. She'll be your best friend for life."

He moved on to the second horse, a black stallion named Bolt that was so muscular it was almost surreal, and started to saddle him up as well. I took the bucket and walked around to face Misty. She was chewing on some hay, and yellow shoots were sticking out of her mouth on both sides. She eyed me warily.

"Hey," I said, offering my hand for her to sniff, like I would with a dog. She snorted and turned her head. I felt a blush creeping up my neck. I didn't want Upton to think I was totally inept with horses, even though I had never been this close to one in my life, no matter how many times Gage called me Farmer Brennan. "Here. Want one of these?" I asked, holding out a carrot.

Misty gently took the entire carrot right out of my hand and crunched into it. Now we were getting somewhere.

"So, do you really think Poppy is okay?" I asked as Upton grabbed a wide black-bristled brush off a shelf.

"She's fine. The girl lives to be the center of attention, and after what happened last night, she probably felt the need to change the subject," he said as he brushed his horse's coat. "She just ran off so that everyone would be talking about this instead of about the fact that I broke up with her."

"She was really upset," I said, stating the obvious.

"As Sienna quite loudly informed me," he joked.

I smirked in response, and then wondered what to say next. I felt a little off-kilter after that errant thought this morning—that maybe I was falling for Upton. And if that was the case, I had to be smart here. Upton was a player, and I needed to know more about his past. I reached up tentatively to pat Misty's snout and she allowed it, though I could see the amusement in her big brown eyes. She could tell that I was a novice and was definitely humoring me. I gave her another carrot.

"I think every girl in that group is in love with you," I said lightly, even though there was a lump of trepidation forming in my throat. I wasn't exactly sure I wanted to let him in on this fact in case, by some miracle, he hadn't figured it out already.

"Not Noelle," he replied, giving Bolt one last brush.

Okay, so apparently he *was* aware.

I swallowed hard. "No, not Noelle. But everyone else."

Upton hoisted a heavy saddle up onto Bolt's back. I watched his arms as he worked, almost captivated by the movement of his muscles. Almost. I was on a mission here.

"Well, I wouldn't say 'love,'" he replied casually as he strapped Bolt in.

He was being very vague and cavalier about this. So cavalier that I was starting to feel he actually did have something to hide. My heart twisted, and Misty nudged my shoulder. I quickly handed over another carrot. This girl, at least, was going to love me before the day was through.

Ask him. Just ask him how many of them he's been with. Then you can stop being jealous of everyone and just focus your little green man on those who actually deserve it.

"All right, just tell me," I said. "How many of them have you actually hooked up with?"

It couldn't really have been all of them except Taylor. Not *all*.

"It depends on how you define 'hooking up,'" he said, turning away and grabbing his shirt off the hook where he'd left it. He offered no further information.

I bit my lip. Clearly he wasn't going to tell me. So I had a choice to make. When it came down to it, did it really matter? This was just a fling I was having here, right? An island romance. When we left this place, chances were we'd never seen each other again. It didn't matter that I was so "in his head" that I was "annoying." It didn't matter that I had almost thought the word "love" in my own mind that morning. I'd had an Upton hangover then, but now I was clearheaded again. Much more so, now that he had his shirt on.

"Shall we?" Upton asked, offering me his hand.

I dropped the bucket of carrots. "We shall," I replied, putting on a bad English accent. Upton grinned, all but stopping my heart.

Fling, Reed. This is a fling.

And once it was flung, it would be over. For good.

SPOOKED

It took about an hour, but my inner thighs finally started to loosen up. It was clear that Misty knew not to take the speed above a leisurely stroll, and she followed the wide trail through the trees as if she'd traced the route every day of her life. Which, of course, she probably had. No doubt Upton had ridden her through here dozens of times. Or he'd had his girlfriends ride her through here dozens of times.

But I wasn't thinking about that. Fling, fling, fling.

"This actually is kind of relaxing," I said, looking through the trees to the ocean beyond. It grew darker toward the horizon, almost cobalt blue where it met the sky. We were headed back up the hill toward the stable and the Ryans' house beyond. Soon we would come out of the trees and head across the open bluff toward the estate's buildings.

"That's because you're a natural," Upton called out to me from behind, where he was keeping an eye on me from Bolt's saddle.

"No. It's because you're a good instructor," I said, turning my head so I could see him.

I hadn't tried to do this once since he'd stopped riding next to me and had taken the rear. Hadn't felt comfortable enough to take my eyes off the trail. Now, as I managed to do it without tugging Misty off the path, I caught a glimpse of Upton's smile and felt proud of myself. Maybe I *was* a natural.

Out of nowhere, I heard a crack like the breaking of a large tree limb, and then felt a jolt. The smile fell off Upton's face, and I whipped my head forward. Misty suddenly had broken into a sprint. The trees were bolting by at an alarming speed and a low-hanging branch clipped my arm, but I barely felt the sting. My heart was in my throat. I gripped the knob at the front of the saddle, straining with all my might to keep from falling off. Pain radiated through my butt and up my back as I was flung up and down, losing my form completely.

"Upton!" I screamed as we came out of the trees. My grip was slipping as my palms leaked sweat.

"Pull up on the reins!" he shouted back. "Jerk up like I taught you!"

My sunglasses fell off, and the riding helmet I was wearing bounced forward, partially covering my eyes. But I could still see the ocean rushing toward me. The edge of the cliff overlooking the water was only a hundred yards away. Misty was heading right for it. I grabbed the leather reins with my sweating hands and pulled.

"Stop! Whoa! Stop, Misty!" I screamed, yanking over and over again. But she didn't so much as miss a step. We were going to go over. I yanked again and cried out. "Upton! Help! She won't stop!"

Upton and Bolt raced up alongside us. Upton's face was full of fear as he glanced toward the edge of the cliff, then at my helpless hands as they clung to the horse. Now all four of us were sprinting toward certain death. I imagined watching Upton as we went over the edge and closed my eyes. I couldn't watch this. I couldn't just couldn't watch us plummet to our deaths.

Then I felt something glance off my knuckles. Heard Upton shout. Felt a sudden jerk and was flung forward, my face colliding with Misty's neck. We veered off to the right and all of a sudden, Misty slowed down. Just like that, she was walking again. When I opened my eyes, we were headed back toward the center of the property and away from the cliff. Upton's leg bumped mine. His hand was closed around Misty's reins. Bolt was walking so close to Misty that their hooves kept brushing, which made them twitch their heads up and down like it tickled.

The horses were perfectly calm. As if nothing had happened.

"Are you all right?" Upton asked me.

I burst into tears.

"Whoa, whoa," Upton commanded the horses. They came to a stop and he easily dismounted. Then he reached up for me. I found I couldn't even disentangle my foot from the stirrup, I was shaking so violently. Finally, Upton had to remove my foot for me, and I just slid off the side of the horse. He caught me in his arms.

Not at all graceful, but what did I care? I had almost died back there.

We both had. I pressed my face into Upton's shoulder and cried. My chest was racked with huge, painful sobs, but I couldn't stop myself. All the terror just released itself all over his expensive shirt.

"It's okay. It's okay," he said, stroking my hair. "We're fine."

I looked up at him and sucked in a rattling breath. There was sweat all along his brow and above his lip. "I thought we were going to die."

Upton blinked. "You know, so did I for a moment there."

I smacked his arm as he laughed. "You're supposed to tell me I'm stupid and we were actually miles from the cliff, and that I'm just overreacting."

Upton breathed in through his nose and gave a slight nod. "You're stupid," he said, placing his hands on my shoulders. "We were actually miles from the cliff, and you're just overreacting."

"Liar," I said, my heart still pounding. "What the hell happened? I thought Misty was supposed to be steady."

The horses had wandered a few yards off and were picking at the grass.

"I don't know. She's never taken off like that before. Ever," he said, wiping his brow as he looked at her. "Something must have spooked her. Maybe a branch hit her or something?"

I shook my head. "We were at a wide part of the trail. There was nothing."

"Bizarre," Upton said, shaking his head. "It had to be something."

Or someone.

I felt a chill go through me and looked back at the trees. It was amazing how far off they were, how much ground we had covered in those few short seconds. I wanted to run back there and check the spot where Misty had first taken off. See if there was anything—or anyone—there. I thought of Poppy's warning to stay away from Upton. Of her ire the night before, and Paige's and Sienna's hostile attitudes toward me. Was it possible? Could someone actually have set off Misty to teach me a lesson? To try to keep me away from Upton?

"Come on," Upton said, lacing his fingers through mine. "We'll walk the horses back to the stable. I think that's enough riding for today."

"Try forever," I joked, squeezing his hand.

When we reached the horses, Upton tethered Misty to Bolt, then took Bolt's reins and led both horses with one hand so he could hold my hand with the other. As we turned north toward the stable, I couldn't help but check over my shoulder one last time at the trees and the bluff, just to see if anyone was there. But there was nothing except the sound of waves crashing against the rocks so very far below.

GARDEN TOUR

We met Noelle and the rest of the crew—minus the Ryans, Poppy, and Sienna—at Shutters for brunch as planned. Everyone arrived in waves, so I was forced to retell the story of our runaway horse experience five times. By the time we were done with our meal, I was so sick of thinking about it that all I wanted was a nice, relaxing afternoon on the beach. Instead, thanks to a plan Gage had floated by the crew while Upton and I had been out riding, I found myself en route to the Ryans' estate yet again. We were gathering at the scene of my near-disaster so everyone could go Jet Skiing together.

Jet Skiing. Like me and my still-quivering thighs were really up for that.

"Look on the bright side," Kiran said as she, Upton, and I walked out onto the patio where the week's first party had been held. We had driven up together in Kiran's car and were the last to arrive. Compared to that first day, there were relatively few people there. Just our group and Mr. and Mrs. Ryan, all hanging out near a big table covered in fruit and sandwiches.

"Which bright side would that be?" I asked.

"You have an exciting story to tell when you get home!" Kiran said, lifting her palms.

"Yes, but I already have plenty of exciting stories thanks to Sabine," I told her lightly, ignoring the twinge in my chest as I said the girl's name. "I wanted to leave here with only boring stories. Boring, passing-out-in-the-sand-and-getting-sunburned stories."

Upton put his arm around me. "I believe we can still accomplish that goal. Although no sunburns. I don't want to see that adorable nose of yours peeling," he said, touching his fingertip to my nose.

Kiran groaned and Upton and I laughed as we arrived at the table. Gage walked right over to me and smacked me on the back.

"Starting to think you're a cat, Brennan," he said. "Nine lives and all the jazz." Once again, he wore nothing but his board shorts and a smile. Considering his sexual history and lack of an edit feature on his tongue, I supposed I shouldn't have been surprised that he was such an exhibitionist. He popped a grape into his mouth and held it in his teeth, showing it to me for a second before crunching into it.

"Ew," I said.

"I'm serious," he said, grabbing another grape. "I think you should let it all ride on Casino Night. You're, like, the luckiest farm chick on earth."

"Or the unluckiest," Paige put in as she stopped by with Daniel.

"It all depends on how you look at it," Taylor said as she added gobs of mayo to a turkey sandwich. "I prefer the 'glass is half full' approach."

"Yeah, well, no glass or plate is half full for long around you these days," Paige said with a sniff before moving on.

Taylor's jaw dropped slightly, and she looked down at the sandwich for a moment as if the sight of it suddenly made her ill. But then something in her expression shifted and she took a big bite out of it, defiantly staring after Paige as she chewed. That whole out-of-Billings freedom kicking in again, I supposed.

"So exactly how fancy is this Casino Night thing? Are we talking Legacy fancy, Oscars fancy, or Cannes fancy?" I asked Kiran, picking up a wedge of watermelon. I couldn't imagine it was Cannes fancy, but I threw it in there just to show her I knew that the French film fest was the ultimate in red carpet. Something I'd learned after living in Billings for a year and a half with my fashion maven friends. "Because I still don't know what to wear."

"Don't worry," Kiran said with a wink. She snagged a bottle of water out of a big silver bucket filled with ice. "I've got you covered," she added, tapping my forehead with the bottle.

I was about to ask her what that meant when Sienna shoved aside the sliding glass door and trudged out, looking grim. Mrs. Ryan walked over to her and wrapped her up in a hug, her ever-present silk jacket billowing in the ocean breeze.

"All settled, dear?" she asked.

"Yes, thank you. I appreciate your letting me stay here," Sienna replied, her arms crossed tightly around her black-and-white sundress.

"You moved in?" Noelle asked.

Sienna nodded. Her face was pinched with worry and exhaustion as she approached us. "It's morbid, staying in Poppy's hotel suite without her. It's way too still."

"Of course it is," Noelle said sympathetically. She patted the girl on the back as if she understood. Then she made an exaggerated eye roll as she turned around to face us again and grabbed a sandwich. Kiran, Taylor, Tiffany, and I pressed our lips together and hid our faces to keep from laughing.

"So no one's heard from Poppy yet?" Daniel asked.

Silence. The hush felt cold and foreboding.

"Stop this now," Mrs. Ryan said, putting her arm around Daniel from the side. "The island police are looking into the matter, and I'm sure that Poppy will be fine. In the meantime, would anyone like a tour of the garden?"

I caught Noelle's eye. Why would anyone want a tour of her garden?

"Say yes," Upton said under his breath, reaching past me for a plate. "She lives to give tours of her garden."

Why would I humor this woman? She had been nothing but rude to me since we'd arrived.

"Sure. I'd *love* a tour!" Amberly said, putting her water bottle down and straightening the skirt of her fifties-style blue dress.

"What about you, Reed? You've never seen it before," Paige said loudly, smirking. "My mother's plants are to die for."

not a weed in sight. As we strolled along, I made sure to stick next
Tiffany. Amberly and Paige walked a bit ahead while Graham and
wyer slid in behind us. Daniel brought up the rear, walking with his
nds behind his back, watching his mother at the front, as if riveted
her every word.

Like I said—weird.

"Every plant in the garden is indigenous to the Caribbean," Mrs.
Ryan recited, clasping her hands together and wringing them. Wow,
this woman was tightly wound. "It's the most extensive garden of its
kind on the island and has been photographed for several botanical
and lifestyle publications."

"Oooh. I'm impressed," Graham joked in a whisper, earning a
punch in the arm from his brother. I smiled. The gesture made me
miss my older brother, Scott. I wondered what he was doing back
in Croton right then. Probably convincing my parents to return my
Christmas gifts and give the cash to him, since I hadn't bothered to
come home.

"Listen, Reed, I never got a chance to apologize," Tiffany said under
her breath as we slowly picked our way along the broken-slate path.
"I'm sorry about what happened at Billings after Thanksgiving."

My heart felt warm for a moment, then sickly as I remembered that
awful night when I'd walked back into my dorm and found every one
of its residents gathered in the parlor without me. The night Noelle
had announced that I'd been voted out.

I almost said, "It's okay." An automatic reaction. But then I realized, it wasn't okay. I understood that they had thought I'd betrayed

I glanced at Noelle for help.

"Don't look at me. I've been on the tour," she said a⌐
some fruit onto her plate.

"Go ahead! It'll be fun!" Kiran cheered drolly.

"Upton?" I asked hopefully.

He laughed and grabbed a soda from a separate bucket
on your own, I'm afraid. No one needs to take that tour mc
once."

Tiffany rolled her eyes and sighed. "I'll go with you," she of⌐
wiping her hands with a linen napkin and placing her empty ⌐
down on the table.

"We'll come, too," Graham offered, knocking Sawyer on t⌐
shoulder.

"Thank you," I mouthed to Tiff and the Hathaway guys. The more
the merrier, when it came to a task like this. Who knew what kind of
accusations and insults Mrs. Ryan would toss at me if I were alone
with her and Amberly?

And so we were off. Paige, Daniel, and their father all, for no appar-
ent reason, decided to come along. There was definitely a weird vibe
in this family. Like the four of them couldn't stay out of one another's
sight for very long. Sometimes I wanted to get away from my family
so badly I locked myself in our basement. Or went away to boarding
school.

The garden was on the west side of the mansion, surrounded by
a copse of trees that provided shade for the plants that needed it. It
was really rather beautiful, with huge beds of artfully arranged flowers

Noelle, but no one had even bothered to hear my side of the story—that, as far as I'd known, Noelle and Dash hadn't been together anymore. That even if they *had* stayed broken up, it never would have happened again. I felt too awful about it.

"Yeah. What happened there?" I asked.

Tiffany bit her lip. "I don't know; Noelle was so determined. . . . She said it wasn't her idea to vote you out, but I think she talked Shelby into bringing it up."

So it had been Shelby Wordsworth. Interesting, but not that surprising. Portia Ahronian's preppy roommate had barely spoken to me before I was president. Then she became my biggest fan until Noelle returned, when she promptly went back to spending all her time kissing Lange butt. She had more faces than a world clock. And with her, whatever Noelle said, went. Although, to be fair, that applied to most of the Billings Girls.

"I just think she couldn't handle being around you after that video and, to be honest, I sort of understood. I know now that I didn't have all the facts. None of us did. Well, except Sabine." She frowned, as if the very thought of Sabine made her uncomfortable. I knew the feeling. "Anyway, if I could do it over, I wouldn't have voted you out. I'm sorry."

"Thanks," I replied. "I'm glad you said something. I've been feeling—"

"Ladies? Am I boring you?" Mrs. Ryan interrupted loudly.

Tiffany and I both paused, snagged. Graham and Sawyer stopped behind us.

"Sorry, Mrs. Ryan," Tiffany replied.

I looked around, surprised at the ground we had covered without my noticing. We had arrived near the tip of a bluff overlooking the ocean. My knees went weak, looking at the edge I'd almost gone over. To my left, the pathway forked off toward a tree that stood all by itself, surrounded by a ring of rocks in the dirt. There was a big *X* etched into its trunk.

"Why is this tree marked?" I asked, taking a couple of steps toward it.

"I wouldn't get any closer if I were you," Mr. Ryan said grimly.

I froze, my hands coming together nervously. "Why not?"

Mrs. Ryan's smile was all condescension. She stepped past her husband and Amberly to stand in front of me. "Because that is a manchineel tree," she said, looking me in the eye. "It's highly poisonous. Eating its fruit can kill you, and simply touching its sap will blister your skin. So you might want to take a step back."

"Yeah, Reed. We wouldn't want you to get hurt," Paige said sarcastically.

I walked back over to Tiffany, hugging my arms, my heart actually pounding because of a tree. "If it's so dangerous, why keep it around?" I asked.

Mrs. Ryan chuckled, shaking her head. "Because my collection wouldn't be complete without it. This is one of the island's most notorious plants." She looked me up and down derisively. "You know, Miss Brennan, when you're visiting a foreign land, it's customary to learn a little something about the place before you arrive. It's common courtesy, really."

She brushed by me and rejoined her husband at the front of the tour. I felt a twinge in the back of my throat at being publicly scolded yet again.

"Wow. She really doesn't like you," Graham said.

He was speaking some serious truth. I didn't get it. Was it really all about Billings? If she cared so much, why hadn't she attended our fund-raiser or the hearing where we were almost disbanded?

Luckily, the tour seemed to be almost over. As we turned back toward the mansion, we passed by a small greenhouse with some pots, bags of soil, and trowels set up on a table outside. Next to that was a workbench with a broken birdhouse on it, ready to be mended, and a couple bags of birdseed.

Thinking about my morning songbird, I glanced over my shoulder at Daniel. He was the nearest Ryan to me, and also the only one who had yet to be outright mean to me—no matter his reputation. "Do you know where I can buy some of that?"

He grabbed a small paper bag off the potting table and quickly filled it with seed. "It's all yours," he said, handing it over.

"Really? Thank you," I said, surprised by how generous he was being, considering his mother's obvious dislike of me. "That's so nice of you."

"It's just birdseed," Daniel replied, amused.

"Are you children planning on catching up anytime soon?" Mrs. Ryan called out, annoyed as always.

"Children?" Sawyer said under his breath as he fiddled with the broken birdhouse. "What are we, kindergartners?"

"Yes, Mother," Daniel called back, ignoring Sawyer's comment.

He took the birdhouse out of Sawyer's hand with a pointed glare and placed it back where it had been.

Daniel's mother shook her head, as if she were fed up, and continued along toward the house. He chuckled fondly, like her behavior was somehow humorous, and walked along, cutting in front of me, Tiff, and the Hathaways.

"Is it just me or is there something weird about this family?" I whispered.

"Oh, it's definitely not you," Tiffany replied.

"They're out of one of those bad horror movies," Graham joked, putting his hands out in front of him like a screen. He adopted a deep narrator's voice. "On the surface, the Ryans seem like the perfect family, but beneath their shiny gilded veneer lies a deep, dark secret. . . ."

"What's the secret?" I asked, playing along.

"There isn't one," Sawyer said, shoving his brother. "He's just being a dork."

"God! Grow a funny bone, man. You don't always have to be so damn literal," Graham groused, shaking his head as he walked ahead of us.

Sawyer blushed and shrugged, embarrassed. He shoved his hands into the pockets of his black cargo shorts and rushed ahead to catch up. I looked at Tiff.

"Yeah. They're a weird family too," she said in an accepting way.

After the tour we rejoined the rest of the group. Upton slid his arm around my shoulders and pulled me to him. I ignored the general glowers of the female population and hugged him back. Even Mrs. Ryan eyed us disapprovingly. I supposed I could add PDA to my list of crimes in her book. But the new Reed was not taking anything for granted. Especially not Upton. Especially not after what had happened that morning.

"Sienna's on the phone with Poppy's mother," Upton whispered, nodding toward Sienna, who had walked away from the group for more privacy.

My heart skipped a beat, wondering what was being said. Had Poppy been found? Maybe she was with her parents in Antigua. *Please let it be something that simple.* Everyone waited in relative silence until she finally flipped her phone closed and returned.

"Well, they're not worried," she said, sounding almost disappointed as she forced a smile. "They say she does this all the time—disappearing without notice."

"See? What did I tell you?" Upton said, looking at me. "Even her parents think she's fine."

"They're not even going to look for her?" Mrs. Ryan asked, her hand going to the ornate gold necklace at her throat. It looked almost too heavy to wear.

"It doesn't sound like it," Sienna said, tucking the phone into her clutch.

"What kind of parents are they?" Mrs. Ryan asked, looking at her husband.

"Calista," he scolded, putting his hand on her back.

"So, Jet Skis?" Paige suggested, stepping forward.

"Yes, right." Daniel looked around and cleared his throat. "I think I have enough for everyone."

"He has fourteen Jet Skis?" Amberly asked.

"I'm a collector," Daniel replied with a sniff. "I buy at least three new models each year."

"Well, you can count me out," I volunteered, dropping down on a lounge chair. "I'm not up for any more high-speed sports today."

"You have to come," Upton entreated.

Noelle stepped up next to him and looked down at me. "You do realize the alternative is hanging out around here," she said under her breath, "with the Ryans."

I glanced over at Paige and Daniel's parents, who gazed steadily back at me as if they knew what I was thinking. I reached my hands toward Upton, and he obligingly pulled me up.

"Okay, then! Jet Skiing it is."

Honestly, I may have even gotten back into Misty's saddle if it would have gotten me away from those two creeps.

SANE LOGIC

Jet Skiing was way better than horseback riding. Rather than being at the mercy of an animal, I had complete control over my speed. Within fifteen minutes, I was racing with the guys, weaving in and out, jumping their wakes. Skipping over the water with the salty spray hitting my face and my wet hair whipping back was the most exhilarating feeling. If I ever won the lottery, I was going to buy myself a beach house and get one of these bad boys. Or two.

But not twenty of them like Daniel. That was overkill.

"You're a bit of a daredevil, aren't you?" Upton shouted, racing up next to me.

"What?" I shouted back with a laugh, veering around Daniel and Paige, who had slowed just ahead of us. Upton shot between the two of them—a rather close call as far as I could tell—and zoomed out to catch up with me.

"You're quite good with that thing!" Upton shouted.

"You're not too bad either!" I replied.

I revved the engine and sped toward the open ocean, daring him to follow me. Of course he did. I was on one of Daniel's older models, so Upton quickly jumped ahead, laughing over his shoulder. I pulled back and turned, cutting a wide arc so I could see the shore. As soon as I did, I became mesmerized by the gorgeous view of the island and slowly pulled to a stop. My Jet Ski let out a kind of coughing sound while I idled.

Just ahead of me was a pristine white beach enclosed by palm trees and wild vegetation. Beyond that were the rocky cliffs that seemingly climbed up into the sky. And above it all, looking like some sort of modern castle, was the Ryan's estate. Upton pulled up next to me.

"What's up?" he asked.

I pushed back my wet hair. "I just wanted to take it all in for a second."

"Beautiful, isn't it?" Upton said. "I've been coming here my whole life, so I suppose I've stopped noticing."

"How can you not notice this?" I said, throwing up a hand toward the shore where the water grew lighter and greener in color as it lapped against the sand. "This is freaking paradise!"

"Freaking paradise? How poetic," Upton teased with a laugh.

I blushed, feeling unsophisticated. But the moment quickly passed. Who cared? I was who I was and Upton liked me. I noticed that Noelle, Tiffany, Kiran, Taylor, West, and Dash were heading to the shore and felt a sudden surge of independence. I didn't want to be the girl who was always tied to her guy. The Billings Girls, former and current, were the people I'd come here to be with.

"I think I'm going to go in with them," I said, revving the engine. "You staying out here?"

"For a little while," Upton replied. "I'll catch up soon."

I nodded and started toward my friends, zooming over the waves. As I got a bit closer to the shore, I pulled back on the handlebar throttle to decelerate. Nothing happened. I blinked and tried again. Still nothing.

"Stupid ancient Jet Ski," I said under my breath. I tried one more time, but if anything, I seemed to be going faster. My heart started to slam against my rib cage as some rocks flew by me. Rocks meant I was getting dangerously close to land. I had an eerie sense of déjà vu. This thing was out of control. Just like Misty had been.

"Reed!" someone shouted behind me. "Slow down!"

Okay. Don't panic. You're in control here, remember? This was not some animal. I just had to turn away from the shore. It had to run out of gas eventually.

I pulled right and there was an awful grinding, clicking sound. The handlebars wouldn't turn. The steering mechanism was locked. I looked up at the beach. My friends were gathered on the sand, looking out at me, alarmed. Noelle waved her hands above her head to warn me, as if I didn't see that I was closing in on them fast.

I could hear shouts, but I couldn't make out what anyone was saying over the roar of the Jet Ski's engine. Sweat broke out under my arms, along my lip, down my back. I was going to hit the shore at top speed. There was nothing I could do to stop. And then, one word managed to make itself heard over all the chaos in my mind.

"Jump!"

I took a deep breath, stood up on shaky legs, and flung myself off the side of the Jet Ski. My ankle banged against the side of the ski, and a shot of extreme pain blasted all the way up my leg. I bit down on my tongue as I went under and tasted blood as my side slammed into the floor of the ocean.

Damn, the water was shallow. I hadn't realized just how close I was. I shoved myself up and stood, turning around wildly to see the shore. The Jet Ski made an awful whirring sound as it bounced up over the sand, soared across the slim beach area, and slammed into a palm tree. The explosion seemed huge for such a small vehicle—a burst of flame flared hot and instantly died. A monstrous plume of charcoal-colored smoke wafted into the sky, and the tree's trunk was singed black. I looked over at my friends, who were all huddled together at a safe distance from the impact. The second my eyes met Noelle's, she came sprinting toward the water and waded over to me.

"Are you all right?" she asked, grabbing my arms.

My ankle and tongue both throbbed. "Um . . . I think so. I think so, yeah."

"What the hell happened?" Kiran asked, catching up. We all waded back to the beach together, where I fell right on my butt in the wet sand, too weak to stand.

"I don't know. It wouldn't slow down. . . . It wouldn't turn," I said, staring at the grip marks on my hands from where I'd dug my palms into the handlebars. I looked over my shoulder at the flaming tree, which luckily hadn't taken down any other vegetation with it.

"Okay . . . that is just one too many near-death experiences for one vacation."

Everyone else was coming into shore by that point, gathering around us to make sure I was okay. Graham and Sawyer were the first to arrive, followed by Upton, who dropped right down next to me and helped me out of my life vest. Finally, Amberly, Paige, Sienna, and Daniel beached their Jet Skis. Daniel ran over and broke through the crowd.

"Reed, thank God. I'm so sorry," he said, out of breath. "I can't imagine what went wrong. I had all the Skis checked by a mechanic. They all got a clean bill of health."

Paige and Sienna hung back, as if they weren't at all interested in my welfare. I could see them through everyone else's legs, whispering behind their hands. I shoved myself off the ground and looked at Daniel.

"Don't worry. I know it's not your fault," I said.

I shoved by him, ignoring his look of confusion, and walked over to the girls. Upton got up and followed after me, as if he was afraid I might suddenly faint and he had to be there to catch me.

"What are you two trying to do, kill me?" I demanded.

Paige and Sienna's jaws dropped in unison. "What?" Sienna asked, her face creased in consternation.

"Reed," Noelle said in a warning tone from behind me. As if anyone could stop me now.

"You're totally insane," Paige spat, looking me up and down.

"Am I? Two days ago, you and Poppy tell me to watch my back, and today your brother's Jet Ski goes haywire and I almost die," I blurted, getting right in her face. "Sounds like sane logic to me."

"It sounds to *me* like your past experiences have made you somewhat of a narcissist," Paige said, not backing down an inch. "Breaking news: The world does not revolve around Reed Brennan. Not everyone on the planet is out to get you."

I felt a humiliated, angry blush fire up my cheeks and burn my eyes. For a split second I was at a loss for a comeback, which annoyed me even more. But then Noelle stepped up next to me and faced off with Paige.

"You threatened her?" she demanded.

Paige and Sienna both laughed as if they were surprised at being confronted. As if threatening me was so obviously the right thing to do, they couldn't believe Noelle was even questioning it.

"We were pissed about what she and Upton were doing to Poppy, so we showed her her place," Paige explained with a dismissive shrug.

Noelle let out an incredulous noise. "Classic Paige. Always deciding what place we all deserve," she said.

"Well, isn't that the pot calling the kettle black, Noelle?" Paige countered.

Okay. She kind of did have a point there.

"Are you sure you were just rushing to Poppy's defense, Miss Paige? Because I've never seen you defend anyone in your life," Noelle replied, glowering. Paige blinked, and I could see that Noelle had her. "Are you sure you aren't jealous of Reed and Upton, too?"

Daniel walked up behind us at this point, sand kicking up in his wake. "Wait a minute, wait a minute. *You* and Upton?" he said, glancing incredulously between his sister and Upton. She looked away, crossing her arms over her chest. Daniel swallowed hard, looking ill. "My God, dude. Is there anyone you won't defile?"

Noelle and Kiran laughed derisively, which gave me the idea that Daniel was kind of a defiler himself, but I didn't ask. Upton, however, didn't seem to think it was all that funny.

"Back off, Ryan," Upton said. "What I do is none of your concern."

"Actually, it is," Daniel said, his face growing red with anger. "When you screw around with my sister *and* my friends, you make it my concern."

His hands curled into fists. My heart hit my throat as I suddenly recalled all the things Noelle and the others had said about Daniel at that first lunch at Shutters. Things about freak-outs and destruction of personal property. Destruction of people's faces. And he'd just gone from chill to fighting mad in about two seconds. I wanted to say something to Upton—to make him back down—but before I could, he had stepped closer to Daniel and laughed.

"You're just upset because you were too dull to keep Poppy interested," he said.

Before I could even blink, Daniel pulled back and punched Upton square across the jaw. A shout of surprise escaped my throat, which was echoed by half a dozen others. Upton whirled around, but he didn't fall. He simply stood up straight again, holding his hand to his cheek. He looked at Daniel and shook his head.

"Very mature response," he said.

"I've got more where that came from," Daniel replied through his teeth.

"And here we go again," Noelle said in a bored way.

I wanted to scream at her to do something. We couldn't stand there and watch Daniel pummel Upton's gorgeous face.

"Hang on! Hang on!" Dash said, walking over and standing between the two of them. He held out his arms and put some more space between them. "There are a lot of heavy accusations being thrown around, and I think everyone's blowing everything out of proportion."

I took Upton's hand and squeezed it. He looked down at me as if he'd just remembered I was there. Then he smiled over at Daniel. "Dash is right. Everyone's upset. We just let our emotions get the best of us, right, Ryan?"

Daniel snorted like a bull and paced behind his sister and Sienna, as if trying to expend some steam. But he kept throwing these fierce glares at Upton, as if he were planning how, exactly, to rip him to shreds.

The girls weren't kidding. Daniel needed some serious anger management.

"Okay. That's better," Dash said, lowering his arms now that there was some distance between the two combatants. "Let's all just take a second to calm down."

"I have no problem with that," Noelle said, gazing across at Paige. They had, after all, started this. "As soon as Paige and Sienna swear that they'll leave Reed alone, I, for one, will be perfectly calm."

Kiran, Taylor, and Tiffany had walked up behind us as if they were our backup. I felt better having them there. Secure.

"I can't believe you're taking her side," Paige spat as her brother continued to pace like a caged lion. "We've all been coming down here together since we were in BabyBjörns and everything's always been fine. Now we're all at one another's throats, taking sides. See what happens when you bring in outsiders?"

Sienna and Amberly exchanged a look. They were outsiders too, after all, but now didn't seem the appropriate time to point that out.

"Look, we either call a truce now and promise to let Upton and Reed do whatever it is they want to do, or that's it. I'm done," Noelle said. "We part ways for the rest of the trip. So which is it going to be?"

For a long moment, nobody moved. Even Daniel stopped walking around, his color beginning to return to normal. Paige exchanged a look with her brother, who glanced over at West. Then Paige stepped right up to Noelle, nose to nose, eye to eye.

"Take a mental picture of this moment, Noelle," she said tersely. "Because you'll live to regret it."

Noelle simply stared back, not giving her the satisfaction of a reply. Then the Ryan twins, as if moved by some silent communication, turned and walked over to their Jet Skis together. Sienna and Gage followed, as did Graham, shooting an apologetic look over his shoulder. Sawyer sighed and went after his brother. Then, finally, West backed away as well.

"Where do you think you're going?" Noelle asked.

West held up his hands. "Daniel's my best friend. Sorry."

Noelle glowered after him, clearly pissed at being thrown aside for a guy. I guess I was right—she and West *weren't* that serious. I glanced over at Dash, who was trying very hard not to smile.

Amberly now stood alone in the sand, her skinny little legs sticking out from under her too-large life vest. She looked at Paige, and then squinted at Noelle, the sun in her eyes. Noelle's expression was incredulous.

"Amberly, remember who invited you here," Noelle said, her voice full of venomous condescension. "Remember whose dorm you'll be living in when we get home."

Amberly cracked a grin and rolled her eyes. "Well, of course I'm not going anywhere!" she said, joining our side.

I guessed she wasn't as big of an airhead as I'd thought.

Gage, already on his Jet Ski in the water, called back over his shoulder. "Dash! Dude, you coming?"

Dash didn't make eye contact with anyone. "I'm good here," he replied.

"Pussy," Gage shouted before taking off with the others.

Dash looked out toward the ocean, his lips twitching. Kiran and Taylor grinned at each other. Noelle had a slight blush on her cheeks as she stared after the defectors. A blush that could easily have been explained away by the sun, if I hadn't known better. Looked like Noelle and Dash were one step closer to getting back together. Not that either one of them was about to acknowledge it.

"Son of a bitch," Noelle said under her breath, like she couldn't

believe they'd taken her dare. Then she turned around to face the
rest of us—me, Upton, Kiran, Taylor, Tiff, Amberly, and Dash—and
clapped her hands together. "Who wants to take the rest of Daniel's
precious Jet Skis and sell them down at the market?"

"Aye!" we all chorused, raising our hands.

"Are you okay?" I whispered to Upton as the group dispersed and
headed toward the water.

"I'm fine. I can handle a left hook from Daniel Ryan any day,"
he said.

"Why did you provoke him?" I asked. "I thought everyone knew he
has a violent streak."

"I know, but he was being a sodding prick. I had to say something,"
Upton said. Then, seeing my confused look, he laughed. "I suppose
it's a guy thing."

"Whatever. I knew you people were all nuts," I said with a laugh.

Upton gave me a quick kiss and looped his arm around my shoulders. "Come on. You can ride with me. I won't let anything happen to
you, I swear."

"I'm going to hold you to that," I said, trying to squelch my fear as
we approached his Jet Ski. "And just as an FYI, from here on out, I'm
keeping my feet planted on solid ground.

CALLING IN A FAVOR

That night, Kiran invited me, Noelle, Taylor, Tiffany, and Amberly to her house for a mysterious get-together. Her home was at the end of a winding road, surrounded by a dense forest of palm and evergreen trees. We pulled into the parking area out front, and Noelle parked between Kiran's and Tiffany's cars. The home was one floor, long and square, and appeared to be made up mostly of windows. Lights glowed inside the house, and I could see Kiran walking around what appeared to be a fashion show runway, lighting candles on low tables with a lighter wand. She was wearing a red jumpsuit with a plunging neckline, like something out of a *Charlie's Angels* movie, and she held a glass of wine in her free hand.

"A runway?" Noelle said, narrowing her eyes as she killed the engine. "What is she up to?"

I felt a thrill go up my spine. If even Noelle didn't know what was going on, it had to be good.

"I don't know," Amberly said from the backseat. "But I bet it's good."

Noelle rolled her eyes. I had a feeling she was starting to regret both letting Amberly into Billings and inviting her down to St. Barths. The more time we spent around her, the more she seemed like a yapping, eager-to-please puggle. We got out of the car, and Noelle was about to ring the bell when we saw Tiffany and Taylor through the window, scurrying toward us.

Tiffany was all smiles and excitement as she swung the door wide. "You guys, I just talked to my father, and he wants all of us to come to the shoot on Sunday!"

"Omigod! No way!" Amberly squealed.

Noelle winced, as if the pitch hurt her eardrums. "Really? That's a first," she said, laying her clutch purse on a tall glass table near the door and removing her tiny white shrug.

"Tassos is notoriously private about his magazine shoots," Taylor explained to me.

"This is, like, a once-in-a-lifetime chance to see a genius at work!" Amberly said, spreading her fingers wide.

"What made him change his mind?" I asked, shedding my denim jacket.

"I begged until he said he'd do it as a Christmas present for me," Tiffany said, tilting her head. "How cool am I?"

"Pretty damn cool," Noelle said, inspiring a pleased smile from Tiffany. She looped her arm through Tiffany's and started toward the living room, where Kiran was waiting. "It's too bad Poppy's not here," Taylor lamented. "She would have loved this."

"Still hasn't shown up, huh?" Tiffany asked as we stepped down onto the plush tan carpet in the living room. Everything in the living room was beige—beige walls, overstuffed beige arm chairs, and a painted, tea-colored china cabinet that displayed antique porcelain plates. The only color came from the aqua and blue throw pillows on the couch and the island-themed paintings on the wall. All the furniture had been pushed aside to make room for the enormous runway.

"Poppy does have a flair for drama," Noelle said, hugging Kiran hello.

A foreboding lump formed in my throat, but I did my best to ignore it. If none of her friends were worried, why should I be worried? I resolved not to think about Poppy for the rest of the night. Hopefully, she would be back in her posh hotel suite by tomorrow morning.

Half an hour later, after some cheese, crackers, wine, and small talk—mostly revolving around the fabulous shoot we'd all be witnessing and what a bitch Paige was—we settled into huge suede cushions on the floor around the runway. I sat between Noelle and Taylor and across from Tiffany and Amberly, who seemed to be avoiding talking to me as much as I was avoiding talking to her. Kiran walked out from behind a curtain that had been set up at the foot of the runway and smiled down at us.

"Ladies, you are about to be *so* glad you know me," she began, clasping her hands together. "Inspired by Reed's serious lack of couture for Casino Night, I have called in a few favors to the houses over in Paris and Milan, and . . . well . . . let's just say we're all going to have fresh gowns to wear to the party."

Tiffany and Taylor looked at each other, impressed, and Amberly let out a little squeal. I still didn't know exactly what was going on, but I kept my mouth shut, since I seemed to be in the minority.

"Oooh, Paige, Poppy, and Sienna are gonna be so jealous!" Noelle sang, taking a sip of her red wine.

"An added bonus," Kiran agreed, closing her eyes and nodding. "And now, I give you my first ever private runway show, courtesy of Chanel, Dior, Versace, and Dolce and Gabbana."

Kiran stepped down off the runway and over to an iPod docking station, where she touched a button and filled the room with a driving techno beat. Instantly, a model roughly the height of Tony Parker came striding out from behind the curtain wearing a gorgeous black lace gown with a straight neckline and tight bodice. The back flared out into a short train that swished as she strode down the runway. I felt like I'd just stepped into some kind of Hollywood dream. Kiran had flown in gowns for us. And models to model them. And if this dress was any indication, I had totally underestimated Casino Night's level of fancy.

So this was what Kiran's wink had meant at the Ryans' house.

Next up was a stunning rose-colored dress, strapless with a full skirt that had a huge cut up one side. The model was showing serious leg, even as the tulle underneath kept the skirt swishing wide.

Along the slit on either side were huge silk flowers, the same color as the dress, flowing all the way down to the hem and along the edging.

"Mine!" Amberly squealed, raising her hand.

"You're going to have to fight me for it," Taylor called out.

"If Taylor wants it, it's hers," Kiran said.

"Why? That's not fair. I called it first!" Amberly cried.

Kiran leaned forward and arched her eyebrows. "Because it's my party and what I say, goes," she said firmly.

I snorted a laugh. Amberly's jaw dropped, and she sat back with a pout. Such a baby.

The next gown was bright yellow with thick straps that were attached at the center of a bandeau neckline and tied behind the neck. It was very different, like nothing I'd seen at any of the parties I'd been to.

I whistled quietly. "Wow. I really like that. Do you think—"

"No," Noelle said, laying her hand on my arm.

"What? I was just—"

"Do you want your skin to look like cat vomit? No," she said again, shaking her head sagely as the model turned around and sashayed back toward the curtain. "Just no."

An embarrassed blush crept up my neck. One of these days, I was going to have to figure out my colors. It always seemed like everyone knew what would look best on me *except* me. "Okay. If you say so."

The next model was sporting a sapphire blue one-shouldered

dress with a layered chiffon skirt. It was so light and airy and elegant that it took my breath away.

"Now *that* is you," Noelle said, watching the model discerningly as she passed us by. "And I have the perfect necklace to go with it, which I will, in all my benevolence, lend to you if you want it."

My heart skipped a beat when the model struck a pose at the end of the runway. If I could look half that hot, Upton wouldn't be able to take his eyes off of me all night. Across the way, I saw Amberly eyeing the dress with interest.

"Mine!" I shouted, raising both hands. "That's the one I want."

Amberly groaned. "But I—"

"Sorry. She's got dibs," Noelle said.

"No fair!" Amberly wailed.

"You're just going to have to be faster next time," Tiffany said, trying to keep a straight face.

"But when I *was* fast, you guys overruled me anyway. I don't—"

At that moment, the curtain was flung open and out stepped a big, puffy light-pink princess dress that I wouldn't have been caught dead in even when I was four and obsessed with *Sleeping Beauty*.

"Mine!" Amberly shouted crazily. "Mine, mine, mine!"

The rest of us laughed as she sat back down, looking quite satisfied with herself. I was fairly certain that no one else wanted the dress.

"This was an amazing idea," Noelle said to me, taking a sip of her wine. "Kiran has totally outdone herself."

"Seriously. I really *am* glad I know her now," I joked.

Noelle smiled in a satisfied way. "It gives a whole new meaning to the term 'friends with benefits.'"

"Yes, it does," I said, grinning at the thought of the many benefits I was sure to reap when Upton saw me in my new couture gown.

FIGMENT

I awoke the next morning to the sound of my sweetly singing bird, the waves crashing in the background, a stiff breeze rustling the reedy leaves on the palm trees outside my window . . . and thoughts of Croton. It was Saturday morning—the last Saturday before Christmas—so right about then my father probably was making pancakes and bacon, shouting at my brother to come down and eat, while my mother was wrapping last-minute gifts on the dusty ping-pong table in the basement. I laughed and pulled my lavender-scented pillow over my face. They would die if they could see where I was.

I made a mental note to call them later.

Shoving the sheets aside, I grabbed my bag of birdseed and placed some on the windowsill next to the bird.

"I picked up a breakfast feast for you."

The bird hopped over to the seed and inspected it for a moment. Then he looked at me, let out a few chirps, and gobbled it up. I rolled over on my bed and looked at the blue gown I had selected from the fashion show the night before. This morning, we were all bringing our dresses into town for a fitting with the seamstress whom *Vogue* had sent down for the Tassos shoot. The dress would be altered to fit me perfectly.

My bird was still eating when Noelle walked in without knocking. Old habits were hard to break, I supposed.

"Rise and shine, Glass-Licker. It's time for our appointments with the seamstress," she said, going straight to the mirror and pushing her thick hair back from her face. In a very out-of-character move for this time of morning, Noelle was already showered, her hair blown dry, and she was dressed in a sleeveless white dress and leather sandals.

"Okay. I'll jump in the shower," I said with a yawn, lying back on my sheets.

"Reed, this is no time to be lazy!" Noelle scolded lightly. She walked over to the end of the bed and pulled on my ankles, yanking me down across the mattress. "*Vogue* is letting us use their seamstress as a personal favor to Tassos. We can't be late."

"All right, all right."

Just then, the bird finished his meal and started to sing again. Noelle glanced over at the window, noticing him for the first time, and her face screwed up in annoyance.

"That's your bird? He's totally irritating."

"No, he's not!" I protested, sitting up. "I love him."

"Oh my God, you're such a loser," Noelle said with a laugh. "All I know is that if I had to wake up to that every morning, I'd be committing bird-i-cide."

I arched my brows. "Bird-i-cide? Really?"

"Don't judge me. It's early," she said. "Now get the hell up."

The bird suddenly squawked and took off, as if something had startled him. My heart hit my throat, and I saw something move out of the corner of my eye. Something outside the window, down on the beach below. My stomach churning with nerves, I jumped up and placed my hands on the windowsill, craning my neck to see out.

"What's the matter?" Noelle asked, coming up next to me.

"I swear there was someone out there," I said. "Someone was staring at my window, and they spooked the bird."

Noelle stood on her tiptoes and looked up and down the beach in both directions. The bushes just outside blocked some of the view, making it impossible to see very far. "Reed, there's no one there."

"Maybe I just imagined it," I said lightly, stepping back from the window.

But I knew I had seen something—someone. A chill raced down my back, and I hugged my arms. Had someone been watching us? Was someone spying on me? And if so, who could it have been? And why?

"Come on. Shower time," Noelle said, grabbing my shoulders and steering me toward the bathroom.

"I'm on it," I told her, thinking the warm water might help me clear my mind. Make me realize it had all been a figment of my imagination. Because one thing I did not want for Christmas was a stalker.

By midafternoon on Sunday, I had made a serious decision about the rest of my life.

I did not want to be a model.

These poor girls. Kiran and the rest of the models spent the entire day on the beach, half clothed, with men they didn't know splashing water on them. The meager clothing they did have on was pinned in a million places, and the pins looked like they were jabbing into their skin whenever they moved. Half their time was spent waiting and shivering in the surprisingly cool breeze coming off the ocean while Tassos and Tiff fixed the lighting or checked the exposure or adjusted some meter or another. When craft services showed up with lunch—heaps and heaps of salads and sandwiches and pastries—all they consumed was water. I think I saw Kiran eat a slice of cucumber, but she did it so fast I couldn't be sure.

Meanwhile, Noelle, Taylor, Amberly, and I all sat on a flat gray rock in the sand, chowing down on chicken salad and coffee and watch-ing the proceedings. I, for one, was bored. The whole thing had been glamorous and exciting for the first half hour—the gorgeous people, the racks of expensive clothing, the makeup and hair artists at the ready with their tool belts full of products—but really, it was just a lot of standing around.

With all the downtime, my thoughts kept wandering back to that blur I'd seen outside my window the previous morning. Had someone really been there, or had I just been acting paranoid? I so wished I could rewind my life to check what I'd missed, the way I could on the Billings parlor DVR. As two of the models began posing in ankle-deep water, each wearing mod bathing suits made up of skinny spandex strips taped to their bodies in strategic places, Noelle nudged me with her elbow, waking me from my thoughts.

"You can see that girl's entire nipple," she whispered.

"Which one?" I asked, squinting.

"The one on our left," Taylor put in. "It's so obvious. Right through the bathing suit."

I looked away. "Ew. This isn't *SI*."

"*SI*?" Amberly asked.

"*Sports Illustrated*," I clarified with a sneer.

"You don't have to be so condescending all the time," Amberly said, shifting her position. "Like knowing *Sports Illustrated* is some-thing to be haughty about anyway."

"*I'm* condescending?" I hissed, leaning forward so I could see her past Noelle. "Who's the person who spent an entire week talking down to me, tossing dry-cleaning bills at my feet, calling me Glass-Licker and—oh wait, I almost forgot—*trashing* my room and stealing from me?"

Amberly's eyes went wide. "I asked you for those things, and you wouldn't give them to me! What was I supposed to do?"

"Oh, I don't know, how about *not* breaking into my room and destroying half my stuff?" I shouted.

"Ladies! Ladies! You two are going to need to kiss and make up," Noelle said, lacing together her fingers and resting them on her lap. "Because there is only one vacancy in Billings next semester and guess what—it's in Amberly's room."

Wait. Noelle expected me to live with Amberly? In the room I used to share with Sabine? Why not just lock me in the house with the psycho neighbor from *Disturbia* and leave me there?

"You want us to live together?" Amberly blurted, spilling iced coffee on her exposed toes. She quickly wiped it up and tucked the wet napkin in the pocket of her silk cardigan.

"Can't I live with Constance?" I asked, my hands pressing into the cold, hard rock on either side of me. "I'm sure that Amberly, as a *freshman*, wouldn't mind splitting the triple with Kiki and Astrid."

"No way! I am not living in a triple!" Amberly protested. "Constance can come live with me."

"Well, isn't this interesting?" Noelle said, tossing back her hair and taking a sip of her coffee. "Looks like you two both have a reason to kiss my ass for the next few days."

Taylor laughed as Amberly and I glared at each other. Noelle could not be serious. But she sure looked serious. I couldn't believe it. Noelle was pitting me against Amberly?

"You guys! Dad's calling it a wrap! Do you want to take some pictures?" Tiffany called out, her oversize white shirt billowing in the breeze from down by the water.

"Definitely!" Noelle replied with a grin. She turned to pick up her plate and cup, but Amberly pounced on them.

"I'll get those for you!" she said with a smile.

"Well, thank you, Amberly," Noelle replied.

Amberly shot me a narrow-eyed look of triumph and walked off toward the garbage can next to the craft service table. I jogged after Noelle, who was already on her way to the makeup area—two chairs set up in front of huge mirrors lodged in the white sand.

"You're not really going to make me compete with her, are you?" I asked. "I'm a junior. I used to be president of the house. And you like me better!"

"All of that may be true, but you both want the same thing, and there has to be a fair way to decide who gets it," Noelle said as she sat in the first makeup chair.

"So whoever does more crap for you over the next few days gets to live with Constance, and whoever doesn't has to live in the triple?" I said. "How is that fair?"

"It's fair because I'm the president of Billings now, and I say it's fair," Noelle replied. "What could be more Billings than a good old-fashioned competition?"

Taylor smirked as she slipped into the second chair and pushed back her curls behind her ears.

"Come on, Glass-Licker. It'll be fun," Noelle said. "Just like old times."

"Yeah. Way fun," I said sarcastically.

Noelle shot me an admonishing look, and then glanced at the hovering makeup artist. "I'm thinking earth tones for the eyes. Reed, would you mind getting me a bottle of water? I'm parched."

I took a deep breath and let it out. I could just walk away. Tell her to shove it. Living in Pemberly wasn't all bad. . . .

Oh, who was I kidding? I hated Pemberly. And I was not about to share a triple. No way, no how.

"Fine. Water it is."

"With a squeeze of lemon," Noelle said, raising a finger. "*Just* a squeeze."

I trudged past Taylor, who giggled and sang the word "freedom" under her breath. I paused for a second to glare at her.

"What? I'm sorry, but you totally walked into that one," she said, earning a pleased smile from Noelle.

It was all I could do to keep from dunking Taylor's face into the huge vat of powder on the counter in front of her. I had thought that Noelle and I were friends now. Equals. But Taylor was, unfortunately, right. If there was one constant with Noelle, it was that she lived for power, and Amberly and I had just dangled the perfect opportunity for power right in front of her salivating choppers.

THE FOOTLOCKER
OF THE FUTURE

I managed to avoid morphing into Noelle's slave by hanging out only with Upton for the next few days. We went for a hike to a gorgeous, secluded waterfall and explored some frigidly cold caves. We lay out in the sand, occasionally reading to each other when something seemed too good to keep to ourselves. We ate most of our meals on the beach just the two of us, avoiding Shutters and the crew-related drama.

And we made out. A lot. Pretty much everywhere we went. It was next to impossible to keep from kissing him, and he seemed to feel the same way about me.

Being with Upton kept me from thinking about a lot of things I probably would have been obsessing about otherwise. Like the Amberly situation, the Josh situation, the stalker situation. Luckily, there were no more disturbing feelings of being watched. I didn't know if Upton's constant presence at my side had scared off the stalker, or if I had just imagined the whole thing. Either way, I was more than fine with it being over.

Finally, on Christmas Eve, I met Upton's parents. Not because we were at that stage in our relationship or anything, but because every year the Giles family welcomed the entire group and their families to their home for Christmas Eve dinner. So there I was, in a red flutter-sleeved wrap dress I'd borrowed from Kiran, meeting my vacation fling's parents on one of the biggest holidays of the year.

Or was he my vacation boyfriend now? Did saving my life make him my boyfriend? In that case, Josh was my boyfriend, too. And he definitely was *not* my boyfriend. He was Ivy's. So by that logic, Upton was still just a fling.

And my brain was starting to hurt.

"It's nice to meet you, Mrs. Giles," I said, offering my hand to the tall blond woman with a gazellelike neck. She wore a white cashmere turtleneck sweater, black thin-wale corduroys and red velvet shoes, as if we were snowbound in the northeast rather than kicking back in the islands. They even had the AC jacked up to arctic levels, so that those of us who had dressed climate appropriately were starting to get goose bumps. Apparently the Giles family really wanted to pretend it was a white Christmas. At least Mrs. Giles's smile was genuinely warm as she shook my hand, her chunky gold bracelet sliding up and down her thin wrist.

"The pleasure is all mine, Reed. Upton can't seem to stop talking about you," she said. "I feel I know you as well as a character in a novel I've read a hundred times."

"Is that a good thing?" I asked with a laugh.

"Considering that Upton rarely talks about any of his friends with us, I'd say it's a very good thing," his father chimed in, taking a sip from his mug of hot cider. With his balding head; small, square glasses; and full tweed suit and tie, he looked like the stereotype of a college professor.

"Thanks for that, Father," Upton said.

Mr. Giles lifted his glass again in acknowledgment.

"Come on, Reed, let's go in by the fire," Upton suggested, putting his arm around me. "Stop my parents from embarrassing me further."

Mr. and Mrs. Giles laughed good-naturedly as we walked away. That had gone well. At least they hadn't treated me the way Mrs. Ryan had. We walked by Noelle and Kiran, who were standing with their parents and Taylor, chatting and laughing. Noelle shot me an approving look, as if congratulating me on charming the elder Gileses. I smiled back and just hoped that she wouldn't make me fetch any drinks for her or run back to the house to get her a sweater. That could be embarrassing.

"What's with the winter vibe in here?" I whispered to Upton.

"My parents hate being on the island for Christmas," he replied, moving his hand to the small of my back to steer me around the Ryan family, who were standing in a klatch with Sienna in the center of the living room. All five of them shot us cold looks as we passed. Upton didn't seem to notice. "They only come these days because it's tradition, and they don't want to be the first to break code."

"God forbid," I said, pausing by the fire.

Unlike all the other open, airy island homes I had visited over the past few days, this house was all cozy old-world elegance. The walls were covered with ornate wallpaper in reds, greens, and golds. The floor was waxed hardwood, dotted with antique rugs, and the furniture was carved wood and overstuffed upholstery. There was a roaring fire in the brick fireplace with stockings hung over it, and a gigantic Christmas tree blocking the entire window—and therefore, the view of the beach.

Upton nodded and took a sip of his eggnog. "They renovated a couple of years ago and transformed this room and the dining room into exact replicas of our house on High Street in London."

I blinked at him, trying to process this over-the-top behavior.

"I know. I think they're starting to go senile," he joked.

The front door opened, and an older couple I hadn't seen before walked in, the woman shedding her silk wrap. A hush fell over the room, and the two of them looked around, as if startled. Upton's parents moved in to greet them.

"What's up?" I asked. "Who are they?"

"They would be Poppy's parents," Upton said, turning away. "And there's still no sign of Poppy."

I gulped, watching as the Simons spoke with the Gileses in hushed tones. Poppy's mother looked nothing like her daughter. She had straight black hair and a long face to go along with her tall frame. But she did have her daughter's carefree smile. Neither she nor her husband appeared to be worried as they chatted with their hosts.

Of course, everyone in the room was whispering. Someone overheard the Simons' conversation and soon the news traveled to us all.

"Daniel says Poppy hasn't called or contacted them in any way, but she had said something about needing alone time on this trip, so they assume she's taking it," Noelle whispered to us as she, Kiran, and Taylor joined us by the fire.

"But over Christmas?" Taylor whispered, hiding her mouth behind her mug of eggnog. "She just bails on her family on Christmas?"

"I'm sure she'll ring them tomorrow," Upton said, squeezing my shoulder. "She's not a monster."

"No, just totally oblivious," Kiran replied.

A bell tinkled near the doorway to the dining room, and a butler in a tuxedo stepped inside. "Ladies and gentlemen! Dinner is served!" he announced in a British accent.

Upton smiled and took my hand. "Enough of this negative stuff. I hope you're ready to gorge yourself."

"Are you kidding? It smells so good in here, my stomach's been grumbling all night."

Dinner was spectacular. We all sat at one very long table set with white-and-gold china and crystal glasses. All the linens were deep red and forest green and the lights were dimmed so that the candles in the gold candelabra cast a cozy glow over everything. Upton must have informed his mother about the rift in the group, because everyone was seated next to someone they could talk to: Paige and Daniel with Sienna; West, Gage, Graham,

and Sawyer and their families on one side of the table; me next to
Upton with Noelle on the other side, along with Kiran, Taylor,
Tiffany, Amberly, Dash, and their families. Sawyer, who was
directly across from me, barely ate a thing and spent the entire
three-hour-long meal staring into his lap as the conversation
and laughter flowed around him. I was pretty sure he was reading a book down there. I got that the guy was not a social being.
But what about eating? How could he ignore five courses complete with squash soup and endive salad with pears and roasted
duck and honeyed ham and berry trifle? Was he on some kind of
Christmas fast?

By the time Mr. Giles suggested we all move back to the living
room, my stomach was so full I felt as if I might never be able to
walk again. Sawyer got up, though, and I told myself to follow. I felt
badly for the guy. No one had talked to him all night. Maybe my
Christmas good deed would be to give him someone to chat with
for a while.

"Hey," I said, sidling up next to Sawyer as he grabbed a hard-
backed, uncomfortable-looking chair from the corner of the living
room. He had just produced a book from under his waffle-knit black
sweater. *Short Cuts* by Raymond Carver. "What else are you hiding in
there?"

Sawyer looked up at me, his brow knit. "Nothing."

A blush lit my face. "I know. I was kidding."

"I know," he replied. He sat back in the chair, which creaked as
he moved, and opened the book. I felt a shiver of rejection move up

my spine and glanced around to see if anyone was watching us. No one was.

"I was just thinking I might see if some people want to go outside and hang for a while. I think it's warmer out there than in here," I said, not willing to give up yet. "Do you want to come?"

"No thanks," he replied, not looking up from his book.

"But I—"

"I kind of want to read now," Sawyer said flatly, tugging on the hair just above his ear.

My face stung. Didn't he see I was just trying to be nice? I was about to say something to that effect when Upton's hand slid into mine.

"I have a surprise for you," he whispered in my ear. Then he looked down at Sawyer, who was still tugging and reading, his jaw set in a very off-putting way. "That is, if you're done here."

"Oh, we're done," I replied. We left Sawyer behind and crossed the room together. I tried to let my irritation go. Sawyer could do what he wanted, of course. But it was Christmas Eve. I thought it might be nice to see the guy smile just once. I glanced back at him to find him glowering down at his book.

Not your responsibility, Reed. Move on.

"What kind of surprise?" I asked Upton, taking a deep breath and letting out my frustration with it.

"A Christmas gift," Upton said, pausing near a set of glass double doors covered by curtains on the inside.

I gulped, my heart filling with instant panic. I hadn't brought him anything. It hadn't even occurred to me to bring him anything. Besides, what kind of gift would I have been able to afford on the island anyway? Some birdseed from the Ryans' backyard?

"You can wipe the terrified look off your face. I'm not expecting anything in return," he said with a Cheshire-cat grin. "I just had the perfect idea for a gift, and it's so rare that I come up with something like this, so I just couldn't let the opportunity pass me by."

Great. So not only a gift, but a perfect gift. Kill me now.

He opened one of the doors slightly, looked around to make sure everyone was otherwise occupied, and then slipped through, tugging me with him. We now were inside a library with huge picture windows overlooking the beach.

"Whatever it is, I don't deserve it," I said. "I feel like such an idiot."

"Don't," he replied, squeezing my hands. Then he stepped aside so I could see behind him. In the center of the room was a huge box wrapped in plaid Christmas wrapping paper and topped with a red velvet bow. The thing was the size of a footlocker.

"What is in there?" I asked.

"Just open it. I literally cannot wait to see your face."

Upton released my hand and sat in a leather wing-backed chair facing the humongous present. He placed his elbows on his knees and leaned forward, like he couldn't have been more excited. All I could think about was how stupid I felt for being so thoughtless.

"Whatever it is, I don't know how I'm going to get it home," I said, kneeling in front of the box. Upton chuckled, and I reached

up to gingerly remove the bow. I was planning on opening it very
carefully, in a sophisticated and mature manner, but then I realized this might be the only gift I got to unwrap this Christmas and
thought, *Screw it*. I tore into the sucker like I was tearing into my
first pair of soccer cleats.

And it *was* a footlocker. A big, metal footlocker, with no lock on
the clasp. I blinked at Upton, confused. A little stab of trepidation
sliced through me. Talk about a bad horror movie trailer. Was I going
to find a dead body in this thing? Holy crap, had Upton killed Poppy
for me and stashed her in a footlocker?

Stranger things actually had happened in my life.

"Well? Open it!" Upton said with glee.

I swallowed hard, reached for the clasp with a shaky hand, held my
breath, and flung open the top. My jaw dropped open.

The footlocker was filled with college sweatshirts. On the top
were Yale, Harvard, Princeton, Penn, and Brown, but as I dug
through the piles, I found Penn State, University of Miami, Boston College, UCLA, University of Texas, William & Mary, North-
western, Wisconsin, Illinois, NYU, Rutgers, Arizona, and on and
on and on. There were at least forty sweatshirts crammed into the
thing.

"Upton . . . I . . . this is so cool!" I said, sitting back on my heels
with the Miami sweatshirt in my clutches.

Upton laughed and got up, walking around the footlocker to sit
next to me. "I figured that you could wear them all this coming year
and see which one you think suits you best. And then, when you

make your choice, you'll have a properly broken-in shirt when you get there, and you'll feel as if you're already home."

I sat there and gaped at him. I had never received a more thoughtful gift from anyone in my entire life.

"How did you manage to do this?" I asked, reaching out to run my hand over the Harvard shirt's lettering.

"Let's just say I'm glad my family owns stock in FedEx," he replied with a grin. His eyes danced in the dim light from the desk lamp. "Well? Do you like it?"

"It's absolutely the best Christmas gift I've ever received," I told him. I leaned in and kissed him. "Thank you."

"You're welcome," he replied, taking my hand.

I turned around to sit next to him again, and he put his arm around me. I cuddled into him as we leaned back against the leather couch behind us, and we both gazed into the footlocker. The footlocker that held my many potential futures.

"I envy you. All the choices you're about to make," Upton said, running his thumb back and forth across my shoulder. "It's got to be so exciting."

He really did sound envious of little old me. But then, his choices had all been laid out for him. I sighed, trying not to feel overwhelmed by everything that was to come. The tinkling merriment of the party sounded very far off from this back room, with the ocean crashing outside the windows, and suddenly the idea of rejoining all those people felt overwhelming.

"Let's just stay in here for a little while, okay?" I suggested.

Upton sighed and pulled me in tighter, closing his eyes and leaning back his head against the couch. "We can stay in here all night for all I care."

I smiled. It didn't even sound like a come-on. It just sounded like he wanted to be with me. And that, really, was the best present I could have asked for.

THE BLUR

Christmas with the Langes was a much more formal affair than it ever had been in my household. Back home, Scott and I would get up ridiculously early and tear into our gifts while still in our pajamas—hair sticking out in all directions, morning breath at full force, Mom and Dad nursing coffee and hanging around with their eyes at half-mast. After we'd made a disaster area of the living room, we'd all reconvene in the kitchen for scrambled eggs, sausage, home fries, and chocolate chip muffins, then pass out until my grandparents arrived, when there would be a few more presents to open. Even during my mom's crappy years, Christmas usually managed to pull itself off in the same old comfy way. But at the Langes', there was nothing comfy about the holiday.

Following some strict instructions from Noelle the night before, I was up with my bird at 7 a.m., and showered, dressed, and at the breakfast table by 8 a.m. Almost everyone from the crew was there. The Ryans and Sienna were conspicuously absent. I assumed they liked to spend

Christmas morning alone, being weird together. The Simons weren't there either, and I wondered what that might mean, but I kept my mouth shut. I was not going to be the first to bring up the specter of Poppy Simon.

For breakfast, we were served thick french toast with raspberries and powdered sugar. Conversation at the table was hushed and polite as we dug in. It was like we were eating breakfast in a library.

"Is it always this quiet on Christmas morning?" I whispered to Taylor, who was seated to my left.

"It's always this quiet at the Langes', period," Taylor replied. "You've been living here for over a week. You haven't noticed?"

"I guess we haven't been at the house much," I replied, taking a bite of the yummy french toast.

In fact, I had barely even seen Noelle's mother since we'd arrived, except in quick glimpses as she moved from one room of the house to another. She clearly had no interest in knowing me, which was fine. Although it might have been nice to get the chance to thank her for letting me stay there.

I noticed that Noelle's father and Mr. Hathaway were chatting intensely again, and I nudged Noelle, who was on my right. "What's up with the headmaster thing?" I asked. "Has your father said anything to you?"

Noelle cast a look in their direction. "No, actually. He hasn't." She put her silver knife and fork down with a bit of a clang. "So, Mr. Hathaway, I hate to interrupt," she said. "But has my father convinced you to take the job yet?"

Everyone at the table fell silent. Graham and Sawyer exchanged a look as their dad cleared his throat and reached for his coffee. He cast a glance at Noelle's father like, *Do you want to answer that, or should I?*

"Noelle, I don't really think that's an appropriate conversation for the occasion," her father said with a placating smile.

"No? Isn't that what you two were just talking about?" she asked, taking a sip of grapefruit juice.

The two men pointedly looked away from each other. Mr. Hathaway asked Dash to pass the butter.

"Later, Noelle. But I appreciate your interest," her father said. "So, Claire, who has the honor of giving the first gift from beneath the tree this year?"

Noelle's mother, who was sitting at the head of the table wearing white silk pants and a shimmering silver boatneck blouse, her dark hair back in a loose chignon, shot him a tight smile and sipped her mimosa. "Now, Wallace, you know I don't announce that until we're all seated around the tree."

I looked across the table at Upton, my expression incredulous. He hid a smile and ducked his head, suddenly intent on his last bite of food.

Once we had finished eating and everyone had gathered in the living room, Mrs. Lange took out a silver sack with a gold rope ribbon around the neck and held it up. "Everyone ready?"

No one said a word. They simply looked up at her expectantly. I saw a sudden flash of a kindergarten class, waiting for the teacher to begin story time.

"Okay. Someone has *got* to tell me what is going on," I whispered to Kiran, who was seated on the white leather couch to my right.

"It's a system she came up with when we were about six years old," Kiran whispered back. "She couldn't deal with the mayhem of all the kids attacking the tree, looking for their presents, so she lets one person go at a time, and that person gives out all their gifts. When everyone's done opening, the next name is selected from the bag."

"Wow. Fun," I said sarcastically.

"It's a Lange family Christmas," Noelle said with a tight smile.

"I hope my name's not in there. I only got small gifts, and they're just for you guys," I whispered to Noelle.

"Don't worry. I let my mom know to keep your name out," she replied.

"Our first Santa of the day is . . . Kiran!" Mrs. Lange said, showing everyone the ceramic tile with Kiran's name written on it in silver script.

"Yay!" Kiran said, clapping her hands as she got up.

She pulled out a huge black shopping bag out from behind the tree and started to hand out boxes from inside.

"You didn't have to get me anything," I said to Kiran as she passed me a package. "You already bought me clothes and got me a free couture gown for Casino Night."

"I did do that, didn't I? Oh well. Spirit of the season and all that," she said, lifting one shoulder and dropping the gift in my lap.

Once everyone had a present, we all tore into them with the vigor of people who had been forced to wait an inordinate amount of time with a wrapped gift. I pulled out a pair of calfskin Gucci gloves and slipped them right on. They fit perfectly and were insanely cozy. I saw that Taylor, Tiff, and Noelle had all received the same pair in different colors, while the guys had opened boxes with leather Fendi driving gloves. I wondered if Kiran picked out the gifts herself or if they were freebies from some of her designer friends. I imagined it was the latter, which made me feel better about the fact that I'd gotten her a tiny trinket box from one of the arty gift shops back in Easton.

Everyone chorused their *thank you*s as Kiran sat down next to me again.

"Kiran, these are too much," I said.

She clucked her tongue. "You are about to be showered with a ton of gifts that are way too much," she said. "You can't respond that way every time, so just . . . get used to it."

Point taken. I smiled at Kiran as Mrs. Lange called out the next name. "Dash!" Dash pushed himself up from his chair and gathered a few boxes from under the tree.

The rest of the morning proceeded in much the same away, each name being called in turn, everyone shouting *thank you*s and *you're welcome*s and *glad you like it*s. Soon I had a pile of presents at my feet—a Thread sweater, a Tracy Reese top, a set of stacking rings from Tiffany, a Longchamp bag. Amberly gave me a lifetime Carma Card—something she'd given to me once before, then stolen back from my room. I wasn't sure if it was a gesture of apology or some kind of dig (an obviously free gift), so I just said a quick thank you and shoved it in the box with the gloves. Dash got me a gift card from Hollister, which was about the safest thing in the world, thank goodness. He gave Noelle a pair of diamond-and-ruby earrings—ruby was her birthstone. I could tell she was trying hard not to look impressed.

"Wallace," Mrs. Lange called out.

Mr. Lange got up with a stack of white envelopes and started to distribute them. He handed one to Taylor, one to Kiran . . . and then he passed me by. I felt a sting and glanced at Noelle, who looked embarrassed. She shrugged and shot a look at her father's retreating back, like she might smack him upside the head later. Why would her father hand out gifts to everyone but me?

"Peninsula Spa? That is so incredible! Thank you Mr. Lange," Taylor said.

Everyone had received spa gift certificates to exclusive spots in whatever city they lived in.

"You're welcome," Mr. Lange said, lifting a stack of silver boxes from under the tree. He walked over to his wife and handed one of the boxes to her, then gave the next to Noelle, and then gave the third . . . to me.

"What—"

It was the only word that came out. I was too surprised to formulate what I was thinking. Noelle looked as confused as I felt. Meanwhile, Mrs. Lange already had opened up her box and gasped.

"Wallace! It's lovely!" It was a white reptile-skin purse, which she already had slung over her shoulder. "Thank you," she said, getting up and offering him a quick kiss.

"You're welcome," he said.

Instantly, Kiran and Taylor started whispering. I could tell by the reactions of the other women in the room that there was something special about this bag. My throat was dry as I looked down at my gift, wondering what I'd done to deserve a box instead of an envelope. Noelle finally shrugged.

"Go ahead," she said.

We both opened our boxes. Inside were two more bags identical to her mother's. Noelle's was red and mine was a gorgeous rust color.

"Holy crap. You got her a Kelly bag?" Kiran blurted, grabbing for my new purse.

Everyone laughed in a nervous way.

"Wow, Daddy," Noelle said, eyeing my gift. "That was . . . unnecessary."

"Noelle," her father admonished.

"No. She's right," I said. I didn't know, exactly, what the significance of this bag was, but it was clearly huge. "I don't know what to say."

Noelle's father squared his shoulders and placed his hands in his pockets. "Well, you're Noelle's best friend and, from what I understand, you've had a . . . rough time. I thought you deserved something nice." For a moment no one said anything. "Hell, it's Christmas," he said with a laugh. "What's Christmas without a few surprises?"

"Hear, hear!" Upton's father cheered, lifting his glass and rousing everyone else to do the same, which thankfully seemed to break the tension.

Noelle got up and hugged her father. "Thanks, Daddy," she said with a genuine smile. Now that she knew the thinking behind the gift, she was clearly touched that he'd gone to the trouble.

"Yes. Thank you. Really. It's amazing," I said. I wasn't sure if I should get up or hug him or what, so I just stayed sort of frozen on the couch, gazing up at him like he was the real Santa Claus.

"You're welcome," he said. Then he cleared his throat and looked around. "Who's next?"

Noelle's mother called the next name as I wrested my new bag from Kiran's hungry grasp. It was a gorgeous bag, and I made a mental note to write Mr. Lange a formal thank you.

Gradually, we settled back into the rhythm of the gift giving. I noticed that the Hathaways' names were never called and wondered what that was about, but it seemed impolite to ask. Finally, it was Tiffany's turn. She gave all of us photos from the shoot the day before, set in simple glass frames. The one she gave to me was a black-and-white shot of me and Tiffany, hugging each other against the cold as the water lapped at our feet, the shoreline stretching out forever in the background. It was a beautiful picture.

"We both look like supermodels," I said.

"My father, the genius," she replied with a grin.

So modest. The girl could have been a supermodel—I thought she was even prettier than Kiran. But Tiffany was a behind-the-camera type of girl.

"Hey. What's that?" Kiran asked, pointing at a black smudge in the background.

I lifted the photo close to my face and my heart skipped a beat. It was a person. Some lone figure standing up the beach.

"Oh my God," I said, breathless.

"What?" Noelle asked, leaning in.

"I knew I wasn't imagining things. Someone *is* watching me," I said, handing her the picture.

Noelle squinted at it. "So? It could be anyone. Someone out for a stroll on the beach."

"Not possible," Tiffany said, leaning in and holding her champagne glass at a safe distance. "That's a private beach and my dad paid through the nose to have the police make sure no one disturbed the shoot. Whoever that is, they had to get by police barricades to get down there."

Great, so not only a stalker, but a determined stalker.

"It looks like light hair," Taylor said, grabbing the picture from Noelle.

My heart skipped a beat and I looked at them, wide-eyed. "What if it's Poppy?"

They all cracked up laughing. "And what, she's stalking you because you stole Upton?"

"Um, hello? It's not like that hasn't happened to me before!" I pointed out.

They all fell silent and looked away.

"Reed, Poppy is off the island," Noelle said finally. "The *Simon Says* was gone, remember?"

"So what? Maybe she took it out and then docked it somewhere else on the island. Or maybe she just let it go out to sea so it would *look* like she was off the island," I spitballed. "There's no way to know that she's definitely not here somewhere."

"Here. Let me see that," Tiffany said, snatching away the frame. She went over to her father, who was standing near the wall watching Tiff's little sister play with some new handheld video game. Her dad checked out the photo, then nodded.

"He says he'll try to clean it up later on the computer, and he'll see if he can get the figure in focus," Tiffany said, returning to us and handing the frame back to me. "If someone is watching us, hopefully we'll figure it out."

"And that's it! We're done!" Mrs. Lange announced, lifting her perpetually full mimosa glass. "Merry Christmas, everyone."

I stared down at the blurry figure, my heart choking my throat. Merry Christmas, indeed.

AN APOLOGY

Once the gift-opening ceremony was through, the room descended into happy, relaxed chatter. I stashed the photo underneath my pile of gifts and got up to talk to Upton. But before I could make a move, Sawyer appeared, out of nowhere, at my elbow.

"Can I talk to you?" he asked.

My eyes darted to Noelle, who eyed us curiously. "Um, sure."

Sawyer led me across the great room and into the dining room, where all our dishes already had been cleared away and the table had been wiped to a shine. He walked over to the back wall and looked out the window at the ocean. I stayed on the far side of the table, hesitant.

"I wanted to say I'm sorry," he told the window, his arms crossed over the starched white shirt his father probably had forced him to wear. "About last night."

"Oh," I said, my hand on the back of Mrs. Lange's chair. "That's okay."

"I'm sure you've heard. About my sister," he said, glancing briefly over his shoulder at me. "Of course, in this group, you've heard."

"Yeah," I said, feeling guilty, even though I'd done nothing wrong.

"This is my first Christmas without her," he told me. "I think I'm having a hard time."

God. Of course he was having a hard time. Why hadn't that occurred to me before? I walked around the table and joined him at the window.

"It's okay. I understand," I said.

He looked over at me. In the sunlight, I could see that his eyes were actually gray and flecked with brown. Very unusual and beyond beautiful. Sawyer was really handsome. I suddenly recalled how I had mistaken him for Upton that first day, and wondered why the girls refused to take him seriously as a potential hookup. Maybe he was brooding, but brooding was attractive. Or was that just me?

"Anyway, here. This is for you," he said, pulling something out of his pocket. "Thanks for including me. Or trying to."

He held out a tiny white shell on a black cord. A necklace. Clearly one he'd made himself. "You didn't have to do this," I said, touched nonetheless.

"Just take it," he said shortly.

I blushed. "I didn't mean to—"

He glanced past me. Upton had just walked into the room.

I slipped the shell into the pocket of my skirt, then wondered why I'd felt the need to do that.

"I should go," Sawyer said.

Then he ducked his head and walked around the table, turning sideways to get past Upton.

"Hang on a sec, Sawyer," Upton said, placing his hand on Sawyer's shoulder. "I haven't had a chance to say happy Christmas."

Red blotches appeared on Sawyer's cheeks. "Sure, whatever."

"What's up with you?" Upton asked, a hint of a downturn in his cheery smile. "You've barely said a word all week."

"It's nothing," Sawyer said. "Would you mind letting go of me? I'd like to get back to my family."

Upton lifted both hands as if in surrender, and Sawyer quickly rushed off. As soon as he was gone, Upton whistled quietly.

"He's always been standoffish, but this year he's taking it to a whole new level," he said.

"Don't take it personally. I think he's just upset about his sister," I said.

Upton frowned for a moment, and then shook his head. "Of course. I should have guessed." He held open the door, a forced smile on his face. "Well, shall we? My mum wants to check out your handbag."

As Upton put his hand on the small of my back and steered me into the living room, I reached into my skirt pocket and ran my fingers along the shell's smooth edges. Now that I knew Sawyer was struggling with the memory of his sister, I was more determined than ever to see the guy smile.

That night, after private Christmas dinners with their families, the crew gathered on the beach in front of the Simon Hotel to get hammered around a huge bonfire. Apparently an entire day spent with parents, stepparents, and siblings made these people feel the need to drink themselves silly. Luckily, my family was a million miles away, so I felt no such compulsion. Instead, I got to sit back in the sand and watch all my friends get progressively messier, while I obsessed about my blurry stalker and whether or not Poppy might still be on the island.

Good times.

"This is the year!" Gage shouted, standing in front of the bonfire and holding up a bottle of beer in each hand. His burgundy shirt was unbuttoned, but his tie was still knotted around his neck. "This is the year I get you girls to take off your shirts for the best boob contest!"

"Woo-hoo!" Kiran and Amberly cheered in response. Kiran even reached for the tie on the back of her halter top dress.

Like I said, messy.

"No, no, no!"

Noelle walked over, having a bit of trouble keeping her balance in the thick sand, and put her hand over Kiran's before she could expose herself.

"We are not having a best boob contest," she said, shaking her head as she gestured with a half-full bottle of champagne.

"Noelle. You are dead to me," Gage said, taking a swig of his beer and almost falling over from the change in balance the action caused.

"No. I'm not saying *no*," Noelle said. "But we can't do it. Not without Poppy. If Poppy gets here, then I am totally in."

"Okay, Noelle. That's it. I'm taking away the champagne," I said, shoving myself up from the ground and reaching for her bottle. I had never seen her so drunk in my life. Noelle usually liked to maintain at least the appearance of being in control.

"Do not touch the bubbly, Glass-Licker!" she said, pointing a finger at me and holding the champagne out of my reach. "Don't forget I control your living situation when we get home!"

"I would *never* try to take away your bubbly," Amberly insisted, her eyes at half-mast as she tried to hug Noelle. "That's how much I love you!"

"All right! Now we're talking! Girl on girl!" Gage crowed, plopping into the sand as if he were getting ready for the show.

"This is ridiculous," I said under my breath.

I looked around for Upton, who had gone in search of the bathroom with Dash a good fifteen minutes ago. He had promised to come right back so that we could go for a walk alone on the beach together—to get away from the craziness and score some quality time, which would be nice, considering the fact that every girl here seemed to be flirting with him tonight. Blame the alcohol again. So far, I had managed to ignore the giggles and grins and batting eyelashes, but a girl only had so much tolerance for such things. When he got back, he was all mine.

Unfortunately, Upton was nowhere to be found. I hoped he hadn't gotten sick. Upon arrival, he had downed four beers faster than I could have consumed four root beers and proceeded to suggest the limbo.

No one had taken him up on it.

Finally, I spotted Dash wending his way back toward us from the patio area. He, at least, was slightly less drunk than the rest.

"Dash! Have you seen Upton?" I asked, jogging over to him.

"Yeah. He's right behind me," Dash said, gesturing over his shoulder.

I squinted toward the hotel and saw three people sort of lurching in my direction, their arms looped around one another. As they passed under one of the lampposts around the pool, I saw that it was, in fact, Upton, and that he had his arms around Paige on one side and Sienna on the other. They all were laughing, and Sienna's hand had worked its way under Upton's shirt and onto his bare chest. Paige was leaning her head on his shoulder, her mouth tipped toward his neck.

They're just drunk, Reed. They're drunk.

But it did matter. Whatever I'd been telling myself, Upton had become way more than just a fling. I couldn't handle seeing him getting all sloppy over two girls who were not me.

Then, while I stood there like a pathetic, gaping loser, Sienna grabbed Upton by the back of the neck, pulled him to her, and kissed him . . . and he didn't push her away.

Bile rose up in the back of my throat, burning like hot soup. I turned around, found Noelle's clutch purse in the sand, and fished out her keys as tears burned my eyes. I had to get out of there. Now.

"Hey, Glass-Licker, what're you doing with my stuff?" Noelle asked, slinging her arm around Dash's back as she joined us. Dash looked very pleased at this development.

"I need to go home," I told her, my voice cracking. I kept my back turned to Upton and his two gropers, not wanting to see anything more. I handed over the purse but kept the keys.

"Oh, no. You are not taking my car," Noelle said. "Dash, tell her she cannot take my car," she added, getting right up in his face—so close that their noses touched. I saw Dash glance down at her cleavage, which was half exposed by her current position, and he blushed like mad.

"Um, Reed. You can take her car," Dash said. "I'll drive her home."

"Yeah. I'm sure you will," I said.

"Wait a minute. I said no. You're supposed to be kissing my butt," Noelle protested.

"Yes. And I promise I'll get right back to it tomorrow," I said, my heart pounding. Upton, Paige, and Sienna had to be getting dangerously close. Unless, of course, they had stopped to have a three-way in the sand. "Later."

I was out of there before she could argue further. I fled down the beach, taking the long route back to the parking lot so that Upton and his girl toys wouldn't spot me.

All the way back to the Langes', I forced myself not to cry. The island roads were unfamiliar and not well lit, and the last thing I needed was to go driving off the pavement. Luckily, their house wasn't too far from the Simon Hotel, and I was back within ten minutes. That was about as much as my aching tear ducts could take. As soon as I got to my room and closed the door behind me, I let the tears fly.

How had everything deteriorated so quickly? Just last night, I had been beyond happy. Upton and I had spent all that time alone together, talking about Christmas memories and silly stuff from our pasts. I had thought we were getting to know each other and that we'd come out of that library with a deeper connection. But he just couldn't stay away from the Upton Game girls, could he?

I sat down in the center of my perfectly made bed and grabbed a tissue from the box on the nightstand. It was Christmas. I shouldn't be crying. I should have been home, watching *Home Alone* with my brother, eating popcorn and leftover chocolate chip muffins. I missed Scott. I missed my mom and dad and my dog. I even missed snow. Who the hell spent Christmas in the islands? It was unnatural. Didn't everyone dream of a white freaking Christmas?

I tried to stop myself, but I was having a pity party, so of course I had to invite in thoughts of Josh. I couldn't believe that he hadn't called or texted or e-mailed *once* since that night at the hospital. He had told me he would keep me informed about Ivy. He had practically told me he was still in love with me. Yet here it was, the biggest holiday of the year, and not so much as a MERRY XMAS! TTYL!

I got up and walked over to the window, then felt a sudden chill and immediately took a step back. What if my stalker was out there right now?

I stepped aside and stood against the wall, out of sight, trying to catch my breath. Was there really someone following me? Was it Poppy? Had she staged her own disappearance so she could watch my every move with no one suspecting? What if she was still on the island? What if she was the one who had messed with my Jet Ski? And Misty . . . was that whole thing just a coincidence, or had someone spooked her that day?

Another chill raced down my spine, and I suddenly realized how supremely idiotic it had been of me to come back here by myself. Noelle's mom and dad were out with the other parents, and they'd given the staff the night off for the holiday. If someone were trying to kill me, this would be the perfect time to do it. What kind of moron was I? A suicidal one, apparently.

I grabbed my cell phone and ran to the great room to turn on the lights, trying to make it look like I was not the only one home. Then I went into the kitchen and rummaged through the cabinets until I found a wooden block full of nice, big knives. I took one out and laid it on the counter, ready to be grabbed if I needed it. Then I sat down on one of the stools and held my phone in both hands, waiting.

If someone broke in here, I would be ready. And if the Langes came back, I'd just pretend I was getting a midnight snack.

Turning over my phone in my hands, I willed it to ring or beep or something. If Josh called me right now, I would forgive him. If Upton called me right now, I would listen to his explanation. I needed to talk to someone, to hear them tell me how silly I was being. I needed to feel safe. I closed my eyes and willed them to hear my psychic plea.

But nothing happened.

ONE LAST MEAL

The next morning, I woke up and the light in my room was all wrong. It was too bright. Apparently, I had overslept, which made sense considering I'd sat in the kitchen until 2 a.m. when the Langes finally had come home from their party. I couldn't believe that Upton hadn't called me. Had he even noticed I was gone? Or had he spent the rest of the night getting mauled by Sienna?

My heart squeezed and I clenched my jaw, resolving not to think about it. I was done with Upton Giles. From now on, he could kiss whomever the hell he wanted to kiss. I was not going to care.

I glanced over at the window, wondering if my bird had tried to wake me up earlier, and I sat up straight, a surprised shout escaping my throat.

The little blue bird lay on the floor in front of the window, dead.

"Reed? Are you okay?"

Noelle burst into my room, dressed for the day in jeans and a green jersey top. I looked at her, my mouth agape, clutching the sheets to my chest.

"It's my bird," I said, pointing at the floor.

She walked tentatively around the bed until she could see him. Her hand went to her chest.

"God, Reed. You scared the crap out of me," she complained.

"He's dead," I replied. "What happened to him?"

Noelle threw her hands up and slapped them down at her sides. "What do I look like, a bird coroner? You didn't have to scream."

"I didn't *scream*," I replied. "Besides, have you ever woken up with a dead animal in your room?" I shot back. She had no response to that one as she sat down on the edge of my bed. "This sucks," I said, tears filling my eyes. "Why did he have to die *here?* If he'd just never come back I would've figured he'd found someone else to sing to."

A tear spilled down my cheek, and I knew it was possible I was being dramatic. But I'd had a rough night, and this was just the capper.

Noelle looked at me and clucked her tongue. "Okay, Snow White. Do you want to take him outside and bury him?" she offered, putting her arm around my shoulders.

I was surprised she'd come up with the idea, and I whipped aside my sheets before she could change her mind. "I'll get dressed."

"This is unbelievable," Noelle said, shaking her head. "You're supposed to be catering to me, remember?"

"How about a day off for bereavement?" I suggested.

"Fine. Whatever. One day." She sighed and stood up as I rushed for the bathroom. "Maritza! Can you come in here with the dustpan?" she shouted. "And some kind of small box?" I was just about to close the bathroom door when she added, "Oh! And that little vacuum thing?"

"What do we need a vacuum for?" I asked, peaking out of the bathroom as I dried my eyes.

Noelle was just standing up on the other side of the bed. She had my bag of birdseed in her hand. "He knocked this over. There's birdseed all over the floor behind the table."

My chest constricted. The seed reminded me of what the bird had meant to me. How I had provided for him and had wanted to take care of him. Fab job I had done of that.

"At least he got one last meal," Noelle told me brightly. "That's something."

"Sure. That's something," I replied.

I just wished that everyone around me would quit dying.

PARANOID

As always, when we arrived at Shutters, Noelle's parents split off to hang out with the other parents, while Noelle and I joined Kiran, Taylor, Tiffany, and Amberly, who already were seated at a table in the center of the patio, a few spots away from the Ryans & Friends table. I was starting to think that the reason most of these families came down here for the holidays was so that they *wouldn't* have to spend time with one another.

As Marquis led us to our table, I noticed that all of my friends were in zipped hoodies and huge sunglasses. Kiran looked slightly more put-together than the rest—her hair was actually combed—but Tiff, Taylor, and Amberly looked as though they'd tumbled in a clothes dryer for half an hour before leaving their houses. Hangover, party of four?

"Hi, everyone!" I said brightly, loudly scraping back my chair.

They all groaned and shifted position. Taylor folded her arms on the table and dropped down her head with a bang that caused all the silverware to clatter.

"Hey, Reed." Tiffany attempted a smile. "I hate you."

"Pardon my perkiness. It's totally fake," I replied, slouching down along with them. "I may not have been drunk, but I didn't have a good night either."

"And her bird died this morning," Noelle said.

"What? Oh, no!" Taylor said, lifting her head slightly.

"Poor birdie!" Amberly added.

"That sucks," Kiran put in. She lifted her juice glass. "To Reed's bird. We hardly knew you. Actually, we didn't know you at all. Rest in peace." She took a swig of her juice. Everyone else made sympathetic sounds. It was all they could muster.

"You can all visit his oceanside grave if you want," Noelle said, signaling for a waiter. "It's got quite an exquisite view, for a bird cemetery."

"I'll get the waiter for you!" Amberly announced, recalling her duties as Noelle's slave. "What do you want? I'll order it."

"Down, girl," Noelle said firmly. "I'm giving Reed the day off, so you may as well kick back, too. Have some coffee. You look like someone hit you in the face with a frying pan."

Amberly dropped back into her seat, looking like a kicked puppy. But she reached for the coffee like a good lackey. I realized that, compared to everyone else at the table, Noelle was curiously hangoverfree as well. I wondered if some of her drunkenness the night before had been an act. An excuse to get so flirty with Dash, perhaps? Maybe

when he'd driven her home they had finally sealed the deal. He had yet
to arrive at Shutters that morning, and I made a mental note to watch
him and Noelle when they first saw each other. The look exchanged
between them would tell all.

"Well, I don't know if this is good news or bad news, Reed, but my
father wasn't able to sharpen up that image," Tiffany said, reaching
for the silver coffee carafe at the center of the table. "All anyone can
tell is that it's a person and that the person is blond."

My heart squeezed. "So it could be Poppy."

"Reed. We've been over this," Noelle said. She placed her order
with the waiter and handed him her menu. He looked at me expectantly.

"I'm not hungry, thanks," I told him. Noelle rolled her eyes and
sighed.

"What?" I asked, feeling hollow.

Taylor glanced at Noelle, who shrugged.

"You guys . . . what?" I said again.

With a sigh, Taylor pushed up her sunglasses into her hair, and
then blinked a few times against the onslaught of light. She sat up
straight for the first time all morning and took a deep breath before
speaking.

"It's just . . . maybe you're being a tad paranoid, Reed," Taylor
said.

My face was scalded by embarrassment. "What are you, Paige?"

"We're not saying she was right per se," Noelle put in delicately.
"It's just . . . Ariana and Sabine really messed with your head. It's not

totally out of the realm of possibility. The psycho sisters basically tortured you, Reed. It would be perfectly natural for you to be a bit on the paranoid side right now."

"You might want to think about therapy when you get home," Kiran added.

"Therapy?" I blurted, earning irritated looks from the table of adults to my left. I lowered my voice. "You think I need therapy?'

"Who wouldn't, after everything that's happened to you?" Amberly put in.

Like I really relished *her* opinion.

"Just try to relax," Tiffany said. "Don't assume that, just because you've encountered a couple of wolves in sheep's clothing, that everyone has some dark past to hide. Poppy is just wacky, not insane."

I took a deep breath and let it out slowly. These girls had known Poppy a lot longer than I had. It would be stupid of me not to trust their judgment. I could do that. I could. At least, I could when I was around them.

"You're right," I said, pushing myself up straight in my chair, but only half believing my words. "I should get over myself already."

"Reed? Can I talk to you?"

I practically jumped out of my skin. Upton somehow had snuck up behind me and put his hands on my shoulders. Of course he looked utterly perfect. Not hungover in the slightest. He wore a light-yellow shirt, distressed jeans, and leather sandals. The word "delectable" came to mind.

Then, I remembered I was pissed at him.

"Here?" I asked.

"Perhaps we should go for a walk," he replied.

As I got up, I looked at my friends. "Actually, I think I will eat. When the waiter comes back, will you guys order me a waffle and fruit?"

"Amberly. Do that," Noelle ordered.

Amberly's mouth fell open slightly. "But you said—"

"Are you really going to argue with me right now?" Noelle asked.

Amberly glared at me. "Fine."

Score one for Reed.

I followed Upton down the steps to the ocean. It was sunny and hot, with a balmy breeze coming in off the water. A perfect day for lazing around in the sand and swimming in the warm ocean. Too bad I was feeling so cloudy and gray about Upton.

"What happened to you last night?" he said as we walked toward the water. "Why didn't you tell me you were leaving? I would have come along."

"Yeah, right," I scoffed, staring out at the ocean.

"What does that mean?" he asked.

"It means, yeah, right," I said, crossing my arms over my chest. "You seemed pretty occupied when I left. Who did you go home with once you realized I was gone—Sienna or Paige? Oh wait. They live together now, don't they? So, both?"

Upton stared at me, his expression almost horrified. I felt the lewdness of my accusation and wanted to take it back, but I didn't. He deserved to feel bad, didn't he? After the way he'd treated me last night?

"Reed, you can't really think that I—"

"Well, what am I supposed to think?" I countered. "They were all over you! And you didn't exactly seem to be fighting them off."

Upton tipped back his head and laughed, his palms to the sky. "But we didn't *do* anything! It was just a bit of flirting!"

"Flirting? That's what you call flirting?" I replied. "When I left, Sienna had her tongue down your throat."

Upton gazed out at the ocean, obviously snagged. "You saw that?"

"Yes, I saw that. So you can drop the innocent act," I said. "You kissed her."

"Yes. She kissed *me*. For a split second. That was all. I was drunk and I lost my head for a moment. Then I stopped the kiss, and I told Sienna she had to stay away from me for the rest of the trip," he said.

"Oh, please," I said.

"I'm sorry about the kiss," he said. "I swear to you, it will not happen again. And if you don't believe me, you can talk to Sienna. Or Noelle and Dash. They witnessed the whole sordid conversation."

"Whatever." I stared out at the water. Part of me was starting to cave. Who was I to judge someone who had, in an inebriated state, made an unwise sexual decision?

Upton crossed his arms over his chest and planted his feet in the sand, hip width apart, like he was getting ready to square off. "Reed, I've said I'm sorry and I'll say it once more. The kiss was a slipup and I know it was wrong. But I am not going to pretend I'm not a flirt. I am. It's my personality. I've known these girls for years and that's the type of relationship I have with them. You must stop with the jealousy."

"Oh, *must* I?" I said sarcastically.

He gave me a look that made me feel like a child. I blushed and looked away. He took my hand and held it in both of his. "Yes, you must. Because, though I have been with a lot of women, I am with you now. Only you."

I stared at the ocean, my eyes stinging with tears. I didn't know what to believe. I didn't know what to do. Follow my instincts, save my pride, and just walk away now? Or do what my heart wanted—open it up to him and potentially let him pummel it to death.

"Reed, look at me. Please," he said seriously.

I held my breath and did as he asked. He smiled briefly, looked at the ground, and took in a breath. He held my fingers so tightly it was like he was afraid the wind might blow me away.

"I know this sounds insane, but"—he paused and looked into my eyes—"I think I'm falling in love with you."

I completely froze. My heart expanded to fill my entire body, warming me from back to front and head to toe and everywhere.

"And *that* is something I've never said to anyone," he added firmly.

Just as quickly, my heart deflated. Because I had said it. To Josh. And I'd felt it for Thomas, though I'd never gotten the chance to tell him.

And look at how those relationships had worked out.

Suddenly, I was trembling. All I could see was Josh's face. Thomas's face. The hurt I had caused them both. The hurt they had caused me. I couldn't handle seeing Upton that way. Cheerful, devil-may-care

Upton, who had never felt deeply about anyone. I couldn't be his first.
I didn't want to crush him on his virgin voyage into actual emotional
territory.

"I have to go," I said, tearing my hand away from his.

"Wait. What?" he asked.

I speed-walked away from him. "It's just . . . I'm starving," I
improvised. "I haven't eaten anything all day. . . ."

"Reed, I don't expect you to say it back, but you can't just run away,"
Upton said, jogging to reach me, kicking up sand behind him.

"I know. I'm sorry." I stopped and told myself not to be the child I
had felt like moments ago. Told myself to be brave and mature and not
stupid. I looked up at him. "It's all just a little fast. A little . . . scary."

Upton smiled and pushed his hands into the front pockets of his
jeans. "Funny. I'm not scared at all."

Maybe you should be.

There was no way I could make him understand. He'd think I was
being an overly dramatic, paranoid freak. Just like my friends. I mus-
tered a smile from God knows where. "I just . . . I need to think about
it, if that's okay."

Upton smiled, relieved. "That's fine. Of course."

"Good," I said, breathing in for the first time in what felt like an
hour.

"Good."

He leaned down and gave me a sweet, brief kiss on the lips.

"Now let's go eat. That waffle sounded perfect," he said.

We walked up the steps to the restaurant together, hand in hand.

As I made myself breathe in and out, I realized that I felt okay about this. For once, I'd done the smart thing. Not jumped in with both feet without looking. And Upton had understood.

Maybe everything actually could just be okay. Maybe I had imagined the whole stalker thing. Maybe Upton and I could just be together without any drama. All I had to do was get over myself. Stop reading into every little thing. Stop taking it all so seriously.

And I could do that. I could.

As we reached the patio, the door on the opposite side of the restaurant swung open, and out stepped a tan, happy, gorgeous-looking girl in a red sundress and heels. The whole restaurant froze as she grinned and lifted her arms above her head in a double wave.

"Hey, everyone! Miss me?"

My breath caught in my throat. It was Poppy Simon.

POPPY POWER

Right, so . . . a disappearance that didn't end in death.

Is it wrong that I was so surprised?

"Poppy!" Paige screeched, jumping up from her table. She raced across the room and practically tackled the girl into a hug. Soon Kiran, Taylor, Noelle, Tiffany, Daniel, Gage, West, Sienna, and Graham all followed, coming from every corner of the patio. Upton and I just stood there, hands clasped, unsure of what to do. Before I knew it, Kiran and Taylor were dragging Poppy back to the table. Upton and I glanced at each other, then walked over to the table and sat. Paige and her faction dragged up seats or stood around, crowding us in.

"Where have you been?" Kiran demanded. "Everyone was freaking out."

"Even though I told them not to," Noelle added under her breath.

"Oh, I just took a little sail over to St. Kitts," Paige said, waving a hand as she perched on the edge of her chair. She sat straight, her legs crossed at the knee, showing off their long, lanky perfection. "I needed some time to be alone and decompress," she added, casting the briefest of glances in Upton's direction.

"We're glad you're okay," he said, squeezing my hand under the table.

"I'm so sorry I worried everyone," Poppy said, grinning and not looking the least bit sorry. "I actually got home last night, but I thought it would be more fun if I came here to see all of you in person. Have you eaten? Because I am *famished*."

"Waiter!" Daniel shouted. He was standing directly behind Poppy's chair, and he turned around to look toward the kitchen. "Can we get a plate of strawberry crepes and an espresso over here?"

"Oh, Daniel, that's so sweet! You remembered my favorite," Poppy said, reaching up to stroke his arm. "Thank you."

Daniel smiled tightly and looked sort of smug. Like remembering the love of his life's preferred breakfast was some sort of accomplishment.

"Anyway, I met the most fabulous group of people at St. Kitts," Poppy gushed, reaching for the juice carafe. "I told them they all had to come over to party with us on New Year's. You guys will *love* them. . . ."

As she prattled on about Jean-Marc from Belgium and Corina from Portugal and their group of world-traveling friends, I watched her closely. She looked at every single person around the table except for me. Each time her eyes traveled from Upton to Noelle, it was as if there were nothing but air between them. Her story went on and on with random details about snorkeling outings and skinny-dipping in some hidden cove, and I started to wonder. . . .

Was any of it true? Had she just made all of it up with her "wacky" imagination? Had she really been here all along, following me, messing with me, trying to hurt me?

Or were my friends right? Had I simply become way too paranoid for my own good?

"What about the blood?" Sienna asked finally.

Poppy stopped babbling, and everyone shifted uncomfortably. It was kind of a blunt question. Warranted, but blunt.

"What blood?" Poppy asked.

"The blood by your car," Paige clarified in a soothing tone. "That was part of the reason we were so worried."

"Oh right!" Poppy said, blinking. "I didn't think it had bled that much." She lifted her arm to show us a white bandage taped just above her elbow. "I cut myself on a rusty bit of my car," she explained. "The sea air is really no good for those things. But no worries, I got a tetanus shot on St. Kitts and all's well."

Everyone laughed, and Upton put his arm around me and squeezed my shoulder. I couldn't believe that no one was grilling her or admonishing her for not calling. These people had been worried sick, and now they all seemed not to care that she hadn't bothered to contact them and let them know she was okay.

If I'd done that, Noelle would have bitch-slapped me into oblivion upon my return.

"So! Everyone looking forward to Casino Night?" Poppy asked, clasping her hands together. "We're all crashing at the hotel after, right? Like always?"

Paige and Noelle looked at each other as the vibe at the table grew distinctly uncomfortable. Poppy had no clue about the rift in the group. Because, again, she hadn't bothered to check in with anyone for the past few days.

"Sure," Paige said finally. "Wouldn't miss it."

"Yeah," Noelle added. "We're there."

I shifted uncomfortably in my seat as both Poppy's and my food arrived. It looked like a temporary truce had been called. Poppy really did have some kind of power with these people. Was she powerful enough that they couldn't see her for who she really was? Did she, in fact, have stalker potential?

I so didn't want to find out.

LET'S GAMBLE

It was a perfectly warm, balmy night. Stars blanketed the sky above as a polite island breeze ruffled the palm trees but refused to disturb our carefully constructed updos. Floating in the water at the end of a long, red-carpeted dock was a gorgeous yacht, the deck decorated with thousands of tiny white twinkle lights. I could hear ragtime music playing inside, and a round of laughter made its way through the air. As Noelle and I walked down the dock behind her parents to join the line of people waiting to be admitted to the party, I felt a warm tingle of anticipation. The kind I always felt before the Legacy. Like anything could happen.

But unlike the Legacy, where "anything" never turned out to be good, tonight was going to be incredible. I could practically taste it.

"What are you grinning about, Glass-Licker?" Noelle asked, holding up the skirt on her gossamer gown. She had strayed from her traditional black, as if she were making a fresh start. I just hoped my suspicions were correct and she was making that start with Dash. He hadn't shown up at brunch that day, so I'd never had the chance to spy on them. Later I had learned that he had been out on a fishing expedition with his father, who had just arrived on the island. Hopefully he'd returned in time for the party, because I could sense that Noelle was looking forward to seeing him. Not that she would ever say it out loud.

"Just excited, that's all," I replied, lifting my shoulders.

"Wow. Upton has really gotten under your skin," she teased. Her parents passed by the bouncers at the foot of the dock, who were checking everyone's very exclusive invitations. Noelle quickly removed ours from her purse.

"No," I protested. "I'm just excited to kick the guys' butts at poker."

"Uh-huh. And I'm excited to spend the rest of the week helping my mother with the seating chart for her charity event," Noelle replied sarcastically. She reached out and adjusted my necklace for me—a beautiful sapphire-and-diamond necklace she had lent me for the night.

"Thanks again for this," I said, touching the priceless jewels with my fingertips. My heart felt full as I gazed at the beautiful lights along the shoreline and heard the hum of conversation and merriment coming from the party. "Thanks for everything. For inviting me down here, asking me back into Billings . . ."

"Oh, please, you mush," Noelle said, tucking her clutch under her arm. "We are not having a Kleenex moment right now. Or ever."

I laughed as she handed our invitations to the bouncer. He looked them over and gave them back. "Good luck tonight, ladies."

There was a loud burst of laughter behind us and Noelle and I turned to find Poppy, Paige, Sienna, Kiran, Taylor, Tiffany, Daniel, and West all heading toward us in a big klatch of raucous merriment. Dash and Gage walked behind them, their heads bent in conversation, and Amberly brought up the rear, jogging to catch up in her poufy pink gown. I felt a flash of irritation at the sight of Poppy and her teeny flapper-style dress but just as quickly decided to let it go. Everyone was happy that she was back. Any tension or worry about her disappearance was completely gone. Tonight could be the best night we'd had since we'd arrived on the island, and I was not going to let anything stand in the way of that.

Not even Poppy.

Noelle stepped back to wait for the others and I was about to join her, but then I heard Upton call my name from above. I looked up and found him standing at the railing at the stern of the boat, looking all James Bond perfect in a tuxedo and black tie. His light-brown hair was perfectly mussed, and he leaned both hands on the rail as he smiled down at me.

My heart stopped completely. If he was trying to charm me into saying I loved him back, he was headed in the right direction. I started up the gangplank toward him.

"Reed, wait up," Noelle said in a scolding way.

"Sorry. I've got somewhere I need to be," I told her.

Within five seconds I was standing in front of Upton. He looked me up and down as he slowly approached, his eyes leaving a trail of tingling attraction all over my skin.

"Wow. You . . . look . . . stunning," he said.

"Back at you," I replied.

He touched my chin and kissed me as if there weren't a couple dozen parents and friends and deckhands milling around us. It took me a second to open my eyes as he pulled back. I didn't want him to see how dazed I was.

"Listen, I'm sorry if I scared you with all that serious talk this morning," he said, holding my hand. "What do you say we just have fun tonight?"

My grin spread from ear to ear. "I am *all about* that idea."

At that moment the rest of the gang arrived and crowded around us. Kiran looked gorgeous in the black lace gown from the runway, while Taylor absolutely glowed in the rose-colored dress. Tiffany had selected a deep violet sleeveless gown with a skirt that hugged her curves and tapered down toward her ankles. I saw Paige and Sienna, in beautiful yet slightly plain gowns, eyeing our couture with envy, but of course they said nothing. Just then Marquis appeared with a tray of half-filled champagne flutes, and Daniel and Paige quickly distributed them to the rest of us.

"Good luck tonight, ladies and gentlemen," Marquis said with a grin before slipping away.

"Are you all ready to lose your cash?" Daniel asked, lifting his glass.

Everyone cheered in response.

Paige smirked. "Then let the games begin!"

We all clinked glasses and downed our champagne in one collective gulp.

"Come on, gorgeous," Upton said, squeezing my hand. "Let's gamble."

LUCKY REED

Everyone held their breath as the dealer turned over the river card. Queen of spades. My breath caught, but I didn't move. Didn't blink. Didn't react in the slightest. Graham grinned and leaned back, hooking his arms over the back of his chair. Not the most practiced poker face I'd ever seen. Gage kneaded Graham's shoulders from behind as the rest of the guys clinked glasses, looking every bit the high rollers in their tuxes and ties. Graham shoved his three piles of chips into the center of the table.

"I'm all in," he said, giving me a wink.

"Reed, you'd better have something good," Noelle warned.

The boys vs. girls poker battle was down to me and Graham. Winner would take all the glory. The girls were gathered behind me, breathing down my neck. Even Paige, Poppy, and Sienna were rooting for me. Though somewhat reluctantly.

"You can just fold, you know," Graham said with a smile, leaning forward with his elbows on the table and looking at me like he was my private poker tutor. "Then I just get what's in the pot, and you can keep the rest of your chips there."

I looked down at my carefully arranged stacks of chips and frowned in thought. All night I had been playing dumb—asking stupid questions to make it look like I didn't know what I was doing, pretending to be shocked when I won hands—as if it were all luck. And it had worked. Graham clearly thought I was just winging it. But he was in for a big surprise.

"But if I want to go all in, too, I can?" I asked, glancing at the dealer warily.

"Yes, miss," he said, all business.

"Okay, then," I replied. I shoved forward all my chips. "Why not?"

The guys groaned and laughed and high-fived. Clearly, they thought they had me. Even Upton shook his head like I was just too cute.

"Okay, then, show your cards," the dealer said.

Graham turned over his two hole cards. Both queens. With the two on the table already, he had four of a kind. The guys shouted, and Gage and West started jumping up and down like they'd just won the World Cup.

"Four of a kind!" Daniel crowed. "She can't beat that!"

"Wait a minute, wait a minute," I called out, standing up and raising my hands. The guys kept talking as they looked over at me, clearly confident. But the girls behind me leaned in a bit, sensing something big. "Doesn't a . . . straight flush beat that?"

Dead silence. Jaws dropped on the other side of the table as I turned over my cards, revealing the ten and jack of spades. On the table already were the eight, nine, and queen of spades, which had just been revealed on the last turn.

"No!" Graham wailed, standing up so quickly that his chair fell over.

"Yes!" Noelle cheered, throwing her arms up.

"We won?" Amberly asked. She looked at Tiffany. "Does that mean we won?"

"We won!" Tiffany confirmed.

Suddenly all the girls were jumping up and down, hugging each other, hugging me. Even Paige threw her arms around me, so important was it to her that we beat the guys. I turned around and raked all my pretty chips across the table toward me.

"Don't look so sickly, Graham," I said with a smirk. "I'll give you a chance to win it all back later. I promise."

Graham blew out a sigh, watching as I took every last bit of his hard-won money. "I need a drink." He turned around and cut through the group of stunned boys, en route to the bar.

Upton started around the table, all smiles, keeping his eyes on me as he maneuvered by a waiter and sidestepped Kiran, who was on her way to get us more champagne. My heart pounded a bit harder under his gaze, and I felt my palms start to sweat. Playing a long, heated game of poker did nothing to my body temperature, but Upton was another story.

"Hey, Upton," Poppy said, sliding in front of him. She placed one hand on the leather edge of the table, blocking his progress.

"Want to hit the blackjack table? We made such a good team in Monte Carlo. . . ."

She reached up and ran her hand down his tie. I held my breath. But Upton never even glanced down at her. It was like she was nothing but vapor. His eyes never left mine.

"I think that particular streak of luck has run its course," he said, stepping around her. "But thanks for the offer."

Poppy's smile froze, and then turned into a grimace. Upton, meanwhile, walked right up to me and grabbed my hand.

"Come here," he said, whirling me around.

"Wait! Keep an eye on my chips!" I shouted back to Taylor.

"On it," she replied.

Upton positioned me in front of the roulette wheel, sat down on one of the chairs, and then pulled me into his lap. I laughed, taken off guard.

"What are you doing?" I asked.

He reached into his pocket and pulled out a stack of white, one-hundred-dollar chips. "Testing a theory," he replied. He placed the entire stack on the eight and looped his arms around my waist. "Let it ride," he told the pit boss.

"One thousand dollars on eight!" the guy crowed.

"Upton! A thousand dollars is a lot of money," I said, my jaw dropping.

"Yes, but you're my good luck charm," Upton replied, kissing my lips.

Sawyer, the only other gambler at the table, silently placed chips on five different numbers. When he was done, the pit boss waved his hand over the game board.

"No more bets, please!"

A lump of dread formed in my chest as the pit boss spun the wheel. I glanced over at Sawyer, who shot me a hopeful look before focusing strictly on the bouncing white ball. Soon a few people had gathered around the table. Daniel, West, Paige, Noelle, Dash, and Amberly were watching now too. I looked around for Poppy and saw her downing champagne at the edge of the bar, glancing over every once in a while with venom in her eyes. Didn't Upton know I was no good luck charm? Hurricane Reed, remember?

The wheel started to slow. Upton held me a bit tighter. The ball bounced around, popped up once, and came to rest . . . right on the number eight.

"We have a winner!"

"I knew it!" Upton cried as everyone cheered. "This girl is lucky tonight!"

He nuzzled my neck as I grinned, and Noelle handed me a flute of champagne. The pit boss swiped all of Sawyer's chips off the table, and then shoved two tall stacks of white chips toward Upton. Suddenly, Gage's fist was thrust in my face. He uncurled his fingers to reveal a pair of green dice. "Here. Blow on these."

"What?" I said.

"Blow. You're such good luck, just blow," Gage demanded.

I looked at Noelle, eyebrows raised. "I'm not even going to go to the obvious joke," she said.

Gage rolled his eyes. "Blow on the dice, and I'll give you ten percent."

"I'll take that action," I said.

I blew. Gage rolled a six and won five thousand dollars. An extra five hundred for me. I looked around and saw Sawyer getting up from the roulette table, about to slink off as always. I lurched forward and grabbed his arm.

"Wait. Do you have any chips left?"

He looked at me as if I were speaking Greek. "A few."

"Good. Give them to me," I said.

Sawyer looked around at the group, most of whom were watching curiously. He handed me five red chips, worth fifty dollars each. I kissed all of them, then handed the pile back to him.

"Here. Bet on a number. Any number you want," I said.

Sawyer hesitated. "That's two hundred and fifty dollars on one bet. Are you insane?"

"If you lose, I'll pay you back," I said. "If you win, you keep it."

"Wow. Look who's made of money all of a sudden," Noelle commented.

"Shut up," I told her. Then I realized I'd probably pay for that one later. "Just do it," I said to Sawyer.

He took a deep breath and blew it out. "All right then." He placed the chips in a stack on the number thirteen.

"Interesting choice," Upton murmured.

Sawyer's face turned red, but he didn't look at us. Just stared at his chips.

"Two hundred and fifty on lucky number thirteen!" the pit boss crowed. "Any other bets?"

No one moved. No one wanted to mess with the karma.

"All righty, no more bets!" the pit boss announced.

He reached up and spun the wheel. I crossed my fingers on both hands, closed my eyes, and prayed.

Please let it be thirteen. Please let it be thirteen. Please let it be—

"Thirteen! We have a winner!"

"No way!" Sawyer cried.

The cheers filled the main cabin, and everyone around us was slapping backs and hugging and shouting in disbelief. Upton grabbed me up in his arms and kissed me.

"That's my girl!" he cheered. My heart practically burst when he said it. There was no doubt anymore. I was falling for this guy. Big-time.

And at that moment, feeling as lucky as I did, I was totally fine with falling.

When Upton replaced me on the floor, I looked over at Sawyer, who was now double-fisting red chips and looking stunned as his brother ruffled his hair. Slowly, he looked up at me, and for the first time all week, I got to see his smile.

And damn, was it a nice one.

"Oh my God! Did you *see* the look on Gage's face when I doubled down and won? I honestly thought he was going to start foaming at the mouth," Kiran said, laughing as we all tumbled into the bathroom together, a gaggle of silk, chiffon, and lace.

"Wouldn't be the first time," Taylor said, placing her beaded bag down on the counter and fluffing her curls in the mirror. "Remember London's sweet sixteen? When Portia spiked his vodka cranberry with Alka-Seltzer?"

"'I'm dying! I'm dying! And I never got carnal with Scarlett Johansson!'" Noelle crowed, mimicking Gage as she clutched her hands to her throat and rolled back her eyes.

I laughed so hard at the image, my stomach started to cramp up. I dropped down on a velvet stool near the wall and fought to catch my breath. Kiran fanned her face to prevent her mascara from running as Taylor braced both hands on the sink to keep from doubling over with giggles. Definitely the best night we'd had since we'd arrived on the island. Without a doubt.

"Speaking of ScarJo, Noelle, what is with the major boobage?" Kiran asked once the laughter subsided. She waved her black-lacquered fingernail back and forth over Noelle's neckline. "You don't usually display the ladies quite so prominently."

"I'm trying something new," Noelle said blithely, leaning toward the mirror with her mascara wand.

"Yeah. Or some*one old*," I teased, getting up to stand next to her.

Taylor, Kiran, and I all expectantly eyed Noelle in the mirror. She managed to ignore us for a good half minute as she finished plumping her lashes, then capped the mascara before standing up straight.

"I don't know *what* you're talking about," she said with the sparest hint of a smile.

"Oh, please. The Dash-master has been all over you all night and you know it," Kiran said, whacking Noelle's arm. "Stop blue-balling the guy and give in already."

Noelle rolled her eyes as she touched a blotting pad to her nose. Then she placed her things back into her clutch, took a deep breath, and looked at herself in the mirror, turning to the side to check her gorgeous profile.

"I may give him a *little* taste," she said coyly.

"We knew it! We knew you were getting back together!" Taylor blurted happily.

"But just a little taste," Noelle repeated. "Boy still has some intense groveling to do."

"Understood," Kiran said with a nod of approval. Then she turned around to face me, leaning back against the porcelain countertop. "What about you, Reed? Will you be officially winning the Upton Game tonight?"

I blushed furiously and stepped up next to her, practically pushing Noelle aside so I could look at myself in the mirror, rather than at them. "Please," I said. "I've known him for, what? A week?"

"Yeah, and I've known him for eighteen years. I've never seen him like this," Noelle told me, walking over to the door and standing in front of it. "That boy is gone. Like gone-to-Jupiter gone."

My blush deepened. As I dipped into my purse for my lip gloss, my fingers trembled. My heart beat so fast that I felt as if I might faint. All night my skin had tingled at Upton's every touch. My body temperature had been at least twenty degrees above normal. But I kept telling myself to chill. To be smart. Cautious. Because Upton might have been falling in love with me, but he was still a player.

But now my friends, the very girls he'd played with in the past, were telling me he'd changed. Changed because of me. And it was getting me seriously flustered.

"Yeah, Reed, forget the Upton Game," Kiran said, placing her hand on my back. "You've already medaled in the Upton Olympics."

"Really?" I said, unable to contain my giddiness any longer.

"Oh yeah," Taylor said. "He hasn't looked at anyone else all night long. And considering the washcloth-with-fringe that Poppy's wearing, that's really saying something."

"Yeah, didn't anyone tell her this is a formal event?" Kiran asked, lifting her cylinder clutch. "We've only attended this party a thousand times before."

"Last-minute desperate attempt to reland her man," Noelle confirmed. "And as much as I love the girl, I'll be the first to call it. Time of death of her relationship with Upton? The second Reed arrived on St. Barths."

She yanked open the door and held it for the three of us. I took one last look in the mirror, my grin spreading so wide I thought it might break my face. Upton really was mine. All mine. Noelle laughed behind my back as I sashayed past her, but I ignored it. Let her think what she wanted to think. I didn't care anymore. My heart was officially pinned to my sleeve.

Or it would have been, if I'd had any sleeves to pin it to.

As I rejoined the party behind my friends, they dispersed to the various tables and games, but I hung back. Standing near the door, I could take in the entire room. I saw Noelle join Dash at the roulette wheel, slipping her arm under his jacket and around his back. Saw Kiran sidle up to the craps table, where she blew on Graham's dice for luck. Saw Taylor grab the chair next to Tiffany's at blackjack and toss down the last of her chips with a clatter. But where was Upton? My breath grew shallow, labored. I had to find Upton.

Then, as if he felt me searching, Upton got up from one of the two poker tables and looked around. My eyes caught his and the room was on fire. I felt choked up. Like I wouldn't be able to breathe until he touched me. He crossed the room so quickly, I knew he felt it too. His hand went right to my wrist, and my breath caught all over again.

"I can't take this anymore," Upton whispered in my ear. "I need to be with you."

My brain went all fuzzy as one word escaped my lips. "Where?"

His hand closed around mine. "I know a place," he said.

And we were off.

OPEN OCEAN

Upton opened the door to a small yet luxuriously appointed stateroom and let me slip inside first. The queen-size bed, covered in red velvet and gold silk, took up most of the space, and the crystal chandelier overhead tinkled with every shift of the ocean. My first thought was that creepy Mr. and Mrs. Ryan slept here. But I decided to let that go.

"I don't think anyone saw us sneak off," Upton said, closing the door quietly behind us.

"Yeah, I don't care if they did," I said.

I grabbed him and pulled him into a kiss that would have knocked his socks off, if that were in any way physically possible. Caught off guard, Upton just managed to slip his hands around my waist before we tripped back onto the bed together. I laughed through our kiss, ridiculously giddy, and slid backward, away from him, until my head met the huge feather pillows.

"God, you look gorgeous tonight," Upton said, shedding his tux jacket and loosening his tie as he crawled across the bed toward me.

"That was the plan," I replied.

"The plan?" Upton asked, eyebrows raised. He ran his hand up over the waistline of my dress, let his fingertips skitter ever so gently over my breast, and then cupped my cheek. I had to bite down on my tongue to keep from giggling over the thrills that went through my body.

"Yes, the plan. Look gorgeous, make you salivate, lure you to some private locale, and have my way with you," I said with a grin.

"I like this plan. I very much approve of this plan," Upton said.

"Good." I rolled onto my side and gave him a quick shove so that he was flat on his back. "Then let's get on with it."

As I leaned in to kiss him, Upton looked both amazed and impressed. I knew the feeling. I couldn't believe how totally take-charge I was being. But why not? This was what I wanted. Right here, right now, in this moment, Upton was all I wanted. And I was going to go after what I wanted from this moment on. No more hesitating, no more sniveling, no more begging or pleading. I was a new Reed. A lucky Reed. And Upton was about to reap the benefits.

I leaned back, my lips buzzing from Upton's kisses, and quickly unbuttoned his shirt. My hands slid over his perfectly taut stomach, and I leaned in to kiss his chest—something I had never done to any guy, ever. Upton let out a little moan and reached for the side zipper on my dress. I let him tug it down and felt the fabric fall open. Nothing was exposed yet, but the chill of the air rushing in over my skin made my breath catch.

"Come here," he whispered.

Then he grabbed my upper arms and pulled me on top of him. His hand found the back of my neck, and he pulled me into the deepest kiss yet. My hands could not stop\ searching his body. His arms, his waist, his face, his shoulders. I just wanted to touch every part of him. Feel every single part of him.

Suddenly, Upton rolled us both over, and I let out a yelp of surprise as I found him on top of me. He grinned and trailed kisses from my earlobe all the way down my neck and over my shoulder. His fingertips hooked over the one shoulder strap on my dress and inched it down. He kissed the very top of my cleavage and smiled at me. I knew that, in about two seconds, he was going to tug down my dress, and I was going to be half naked in front of him, and I wanted it. I wanted him to see me. I wanted him to be the one. My first. My first since Thomas.

"You are the most beautiful girl I have ever seen," Upton whispered.

His hand slid down my body and then up, under my skirt, trailing my thigh. When his fingers found the side of my panties, I felt a rush of surprise. He was going straight for the goal line. No taking it slow for this guy.

I felt the tug on my underwear and heard a creak. I looked up, past Upton's shoulder, and my heart completely seized. Poppy Simon was standing in the doorway, staring down at me, her mouth agape.

"Upton. Stop," I said firmly.

He must have heard the panic in my voice, because he did. Right away. He turned around and, at that moment, Mrs. Ryan joined Poppy. She was saying something about the new furnishings—giving another tour, I supposed—but she stopped midsentence when she saw us. The ginormous puffed sleeves of her green gown took up almost the entire doorway.

"Upton? What are you doing in here?" Mrs. Ryan said automatically.

Then I saw her take in the scene. Me clinging to my unzipped dress. Upton with his shirt wide open, his tie and jacket on the floor. I pretty much wanted to die. Poppy burst into tears before turning around and running up the steps to the main deck. I could hear her wailing all the way back to the party. Mrs. Ryan's face set into a hard, cold frown.

"Upton Giles," she said in a shaky voice. "I would have thought that a young man with your upbringing would have a bit more discretion."

Upton swung his legs around the side of the bed and bent to pick up his jacket. "I apologize, Mrs. Ryan. We were just—"

"I know what you were doing," she replied.

With a huge lump in my throat, I slid off the bed and hastily zipped up my dress. Thank God that was all I had to do. But the very idea of walking past Mrs. Ryan in the tiny space between her and the door was horrifying, I couldn't make myself do it. Couldn't make myself move. There was such ferocity in the woman's light eyes that I thought she might pounce on top of me and tear my hair out.

"Mrs. Ryan, I'm so sorry," I stammered. "I don't know what to say. I—"

"Kindly save your whorish excuses for someone who cares," Mrs. Ryan said through her teeth. Then she stepped out into the hallway and slammed the door. "When I come back here in five minutes, Upton, I expect this room to be empty," she called from the other side. I heard her organza dress swishing behind her as she stormed up the stairs.

"Omigod," I said breathlessly, doubling over. "I have never been so embarrassed in my entire life."

Upton walked over to me, shrugging into his jacket. I expected him to put his arms around me and comfort me. Tell me Mrs. Ryan would forget all about it and that stuff like this happened all the time. But instead, he quickly retied his tie and cleared his throat, squaring his shoulders.

"Reed, I'm sorry, but I have to go take care of something," he said in a formal tone. "I'll meet you back at the party."

"Wait. What? What are you taking care of?" I asked. Then I looked at the closed door. "You don't mean Poppy."

His jaw clenched. "I really must go."

"Wait. Upton—"

He grasped my shoulders, planted a kiss on my forehead, and leaned back. "We'll talk later." Then he took off at a jog, leaving the door yawning open behind him.

I collapsed back against the wall, looked up at the ceiling, and laughed. Laughed a nice, big, bitter laugh. Of course he had to go after Poppy. Of course he did. What was wrong with him? He had told me he was falling in love with me. If that was the case, then how could he strand me here like this at the most mortifying moment of my life? How?

Answer: He was programmed to take care of his own. These people had been his friends—practically his family—for life. No matter how he thought he felt about me, I would never measure up to them. A chill ran over my body, and I hugged my goose-pimpled skin. Somehow, I always ended up alone.

I turned and trudged up the stairs, but I paused just outside the doorway to the main cabin and the party. There was no way I could go in there right now and face my friends and all their leading questions. There was no way I could watch as Upton begged for Poppy's forgiveness. I was on a boat in the middle of the ocean, so there was no real escape, but I could at least take a few minutes to myself.

I turned right and walked outside onto the deck that ran all the way around the yacht. As I strolled along the freshly waxed planks toward the stern, I couldn't help but feel abominably stupid for even trying to wrest Upton away from his incestuous crowd. Clearly, this life-long bond among them was way deeper than I had ever understood. Poppy's feelings obviously meant more to him than mine did, and probably they always would. Maybe he had said he loved me, but he had no idea what that meant. Not in the real world.

I paused at the very rear of the boat and looked out across the black ocean. We were on our way back to shore now, thank God, but we were far out enough that homes along the beach looked like pastel doll-houses. All that spread before me were miles and miles of endless water. I took a deep breath and told myself to let Upton go. Leave him out here on the open ocean and never look back.

But I kept seeing his face. His smile. That ridiculously sexy glint in his eyes. The way he'd looked at me when I'd first arrived at the party tonight. The way he'd grinned like a little boy when I'd opened my Christmas gift. I could feel his arms around me, his hands on my skin, his fingers in my hair. I had a serious problem here.

I had fallen for a player.

I leaned against the railing and sighed. An odd sort of musky scent filled my nostrils. Before I even could think about where it might have come from, I felt a tug on my necklace and, for a fleeting moment, lost the ability to breathe. Then a pair of hands hit me squarely in the back and shoved. Hard. The necklace cut into my skin as it was torn from my neck. I let out a surprised shout and felt my shoes slip on the slick deck. My heart jumped into my throat as my stomach swooped up into my chest. I grabbed for the railing, but it was no good. I was already falling. A scream escaped my throat, but it was drowned out by the grinding engines and churning water.

One thought wildly repeated itself in my mind during the two seconds it took me to plunge into the ocean. Someone had pushed me. Someone had pushed me. Someone was trying to kill me.

The last thing I heard before I hit the cold, dark water was the sound of gleeful squealing and cheering, as someone at the tables won big.

Some girls would die
for a life of Privilege . . .
Some would even kill for it.

Don't miss a minute of this delectably naughty series by bestselling author Kate Brian.

Available
Now

Available
June 2009

Yachts, premieres, couture . . .

When you're this big,

those are the little things in life.

The Girl series

Girl Stays in the Picture
June 2009

Check out the first book in the new series
from the bestselling author of
The Au Pairs and *Blue Bloods*.